BURN SO GOOD

Into The Fire Series

J.H. CROIX

J.H. CROIX

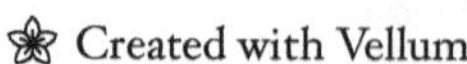 Created with Vellum

To all of us who carry scars for they only make us stronger.

Sign up for my newsletter for information on new releases & get a FREE copy of one of my books!

http://jhcroixauthor.com/subscribe/

Follow me!
jhcroix@jhcroix.com
https://amazon.com/author/jhcroix
https://www.bookbub.com/authors/j-h-croix
https://www.facebook.com/jhcroix

BURN SO GOOD

Caleb

Ella meant *everything* to me once. We were young and foolish when tragedy tore us apart.

She went running, and I was too torn up to chase after her and make it right. They say time heals all wounds.

Some things never die, and the fire between us burns hotter than ever. I'll do anything to keep her safe, to make her mine.

Ella

I said goodbye to Caleb ten years ago. The boy I once loved is a man now—a rugged, handsome as h*ll man.

We lost almost everything once. As a hotshot firefighter, he's all about saving others. Life ripped us apart, stealing more than I could've imagined.

Once again, he comes to my rescue. This time, I'm running from a different set of demons. Maybe this time we have a second chance.

*This is a full-length standalone romance with a guaranteed happily-ever-after.

Chapter One

CALEB

The chilly rain pelted against my face as I leapt out of the truck. Dashing across the highway, I hurried around the car lying on its side in the ditch. The driver's side was crumpled, and I couldn't get a good look at the driver. "Hello? Say something if you can hear me," I called.

Nothing but the sound of the rain drumming on the car answered me.

With my heart pounding out a staccato beat, I scanned the scene. The ground was muddy and slick. If I was going to have any luck checking on the driver and getting whoever it was out, I'd have to climb on top of the vehicle, which happened to be the passenger side at the moment. Oblivious to the rain, I rounded the wrecked car and pulled myself up. The passenger side window was broken, so I carefully knocked the glass loose to the ground and glanced through.

"Hey..."

My words clogged up in my throat, and my heart took off like a rocket. Ella Masters was in a crumpled ball, mostly toward the dashboard. A trickle of blood ran from her forehead down her cheek. I had to force myself to stay focused. This went from a routine rescue to something far too personal the second I laid eyes on her.

"Ella, Ella!"

I tried to keep my voice calm, but I could feel the sense of panic rising inside. When she didn't reply, I almost did something stupid and started to crawl through the window. A jagged edge of torn metal caught the sleeve of my jacket, nudging me enough to shake free of the panic.

Pausing, I took stock. Reaching through the window, I rested two fingertips against Ella's wrist where it lay limply on the steering wheel. I breathed a sigh of relief when I felt her pulse. The nightmarish feeling inside subsided marginally. I still needed to get her out, but at least I knew she was alive.

Fumbling in my pocket, I yanked my cellphone out, quickly making a call.

"Nine-one-one, what's your emergency?"

"Hey Maisie, it's Caleb. Accident out on the highway."

"Already paging the crew on duty. I'm confirming your location now," Maisie replied swiftly. "Anything I need to tell them?"

"Just that it's Ella Masters. You might want to give Cade a heads up if he's headed this way," I said, referring to Ella's older brother who happened to work with me at Willow Brook Fire & Rescue.

"Is she okay?" Maisie asked calmly.

Looking over at Ella's face, my heart clenched and panic gripped my chest like a vise. Pushing back against it, I swallowed. "She's got a pulse, but she's unconscious." Scanning her over, I absorbed the details. She had a bleeding gash along her hairline and her body was tucked up toward the roof. By some miracle, I didn't see any other injuries, although I couldn't see too much. Cool rain was falling through the broken window. Her face was damp and her skin was turning bluish.

"You have my location?" I asked Maisie, the ever-reliable dispatcher for our station.

"Of course. Crew's about three minutes away. It's Beck's team. I'll give Cade a call to let him know," she said softly.

"Okay. I'm gonna go. I think I can get her out of the vehicle. Bye."

"Be…"

I assumed she meant to tell me to be careful, but I didn't wait to hear it. Worry didn't even capture what was galloping through my thoughts. My singular focus was to get Ella safely out of here.

Stuffing my phone back in my pocket, I took a steadying breath and then carefully stepped back. With my feet on the back door, I managed to open the other door. Moving carefully, I wedged my hips against the door to hold it open and reached in for Ella.

The moment I curled my hands around both of hers, I nearly lost my balance when she spoke. "Caleb?"

My eyes whipped to her face. Her wide green eyes met mine, hazy and confused. "What happened? Why are you here?"

I was so damn relieved she was conscious, emotion tightened in my chest. "You had an accident. I was driving back from Anchorage and stopped to check on the car. An emergency team is on the way, but I'm trying to see if we can get you out of here first. How do you feel?"

Ella stared at me, and it felt as if I was spinning back in time to the most terrifying night of my life. With a hard mental shake, I forced myself to focus.

"I think I'm okay. I must've hit my head," she murmured as she lifted her hand and brushed at the streak of blood on her cheek.

Blood didn't usually get to me. At all. But this was Ella. I could hardly stand to think about her being injured.

"Anything else hurt?"

She started to move, and I tightened my grip on her

wrist, my heart thudding hard and fast against my ribs. "Wait. First let me know how you feel."

Her gaze met mine again. If I got through this without having a heart attack, it'd be a damn miracle.

"I think I'm fine. Let me..."

"Ella! Take it slow," I said abruptly when she started to scramble out from where she was pinned.

"Still bossy, I see," she said with a wobbly smile.

I had just about gotten a grip on myself. Hell, I was a hotshot firefighter. Assisting someone in a car accident was all in a day's work for me. Or should've been. But this was Ella, and we had history—messy history that included another car accident, one that tore us apart. The moment a tear rolled down her cheek, I was done for.

"Ella, don't cry," I managed over the tightness in my throat. "You're gonna be fine. Move slowly, and we'll get you out of here."

As if fate was shining a ray on us, the rain lightened up slightly. The next few minutes were a jumble. I managed to help Ella out of the car, right about the time the emergency crew arrived.

Beck Steele, who I'd known since we were in elementary school, all but shoved me out of the way when he realized who I'd helped out of the car. Beck headed up one of the crews at Willow Brook Fire & Rescue, while I was a foreman on another crew. Ella's older brother Cade headed up yet another crew. It was a bittersweet reality to work with Ella's older brother.

All of that spun through my mind while Beck started directing his crew to deal with Ella's likely totaled car. "You're damn lucky she was okay to pull out," he muttered in my ear after she was escorted over to the ambulance to get checked out by the EMT's.

"Fuck off," I mumbled. "You'd have done the same damn thing. I checked on her first. As you can see, she was safe to get out of the vehicle."

Beck rested a hand on his hip, swatting at the rain falling from the sky as if he could make it stop. "I probably would've," he said after a beat. "You know if Maisie called Cade?"

"She said she would. I'll..."

Beck shook his head sharply. "Don't call him. Let Maisie take care of it. She'll be online with the EMT's to give him the latest update." Someone called his name. With a quick nod to me, he turned.

Watching him walk away, I spun around and strode to the ambulance. Ella was seated on the back edge. Reaching her side, I paused in front of her. "You okay?"

My heart kicked up a notch just being close to her. It had been five years since I'd seen Ella. She looked up at me through the rain, her green eyes bright in the gray light. I felt as if I was spinning back in time—emotions jostling against each other in the process. I'd loved Ella fiercely once upon a time.

"I think so. Dana said I just need a few stitches, right?" she asked, her gaze swinging to Dana Halloran, one of the EMT's on the scene.

Dana nodded from where she stood, turning back to Ella, her eyes bouncing between us briefly. She squirted disinfectant on a cotton ball, carefully dabbing at the cut on the side of Ella's forehead. "That looks like all you'll need. I'll just clean this up and we'll get going. They'll take care of the stitches at the hospital."

Ella looked back at me. "See, just a few stitches."

"I'll meet you at the hospital," I said as Dana carefully taped a piece of gauze over the cut.

"You don't need to do that," Ella replied.

Dana stepped away and spoke to the ambulance driver. I focused on Ella. "I'll meet you there," I repeated.

"Caleb, you don't have to take care of me. I'm..."

A flash of anger rose inside. I might not have been

thinking too clearly, but for God's sake. Ella had once meant everything to me. Then, everything went to hell.

"Ella, you just had a car accident. Is it absolutely necessary to act like we mean nothing to each other?"

Chapter Two

ELLA

Waiting in the cold room, I hugged my arms around my waist, trying to will the chill away. I was tired, so very tired. I was also cold and damp. My emotions were pressing against my skin. I wanted to hold them in, but I was all out of strength. I felt ragged and raw. Of all the things to happen today, I had a stupid car accident. I was so close to home, so anxious to get there, I hadn't been paying attention to how fast I was going. I took that corner on the highway and skidded out of control on the slick surface of the road, my car tumbling into the ditch.

And who showed up to rescue me? Caleb Fox. The one and only man I'd never forgotten. What were the chances? To say our history was messy didn't quite capture it. Today was the second time in my life Caleb had pulled me out of a wrecked car. The last time, the car had been on fire, and I'd almost died. Yet, I'd been lucky. Caleb's best friend had died in that same accident.

I didn't realize I was crying until I felt the hot tears rolling down my cheeks. Spinning around, I grabbed a tissue from the box on the counter running along the wall. This room felt so oddly familiar, probably because I'd spent three weeks in the hospital after that last accident. Hospitals had a weird, cold, sterile feeling to them. It was strangely comforting to me.

My stitches were done, and I was ready to go, but they told me to wait until the nurse returned to clear me for discharge. With the tissue balled in my hand, I let myself cry for a few minutes. I was all alone, literally and figuratively.

Leaning my hips against the table, I sobbed. I was running home, and I'd been so desperate to get here, I'd completely forgotten to consider that Caleb might be around. Sobs wracked my shoulders, and my head ached from whatever I'd banged into when my car rolled into the ditch.

Get it together, Ella. It's no biggie. You and Caleb have a past, but that's all it is. You can face him. After what you've been through lately, you can handle this.

On the heels of a shuddering breath, I wiped my tears away and tossed the tissue in the wastebasket by the door.

There was a soft knock on the door. Assuming it was the nurse coming to tell me I could finally leave, I called out, "Come in."

Instead of the nurse, Caleb stepped through the door. The moment I laid eyes on him, my pulse lunged. Somehow, I'd forgotten how ridiculously handsome he was. He had straight brown hair that he kept cropped close to his head with chocolate brown eyes. My eyes coasted over him, absorbing the sight of his familiar face with its clean lines—a strong, square jaw, full lips, cheekbones that looked sculpted from stone, and a blade of a nose. As if his face wasn't enough, he had a body of pure muscle. In his faded jeans and damp T-shirt, not much was hidden. The fabric caressed him the way my hands itched to do so.

"Hey, just stopped by to check on you," he said, his voice like honeyed whiskey.

Tears pricked at the backs of my eyes, but I swallowed,

forcing the emotion away. I would *not* fall apart in front of him.

"Hey," I croaked.

The room wasn't very big, so when he took a few steps, he was right in front of me. Oh geez. I could smell him—that crisp scent of spruce he seemed to carry with him. I took a deep breath, by force of will keeping my eyes on him.

"How do you feel?" he asked, stuffing his hands in his pockets.

Tightening my arms around my waist, I shrugged. "Fine. They stitched me up and said I'd be cleared to go soon. I'm just waiting, but it's taking forever."

He nodded, his eyes scanning me. This was so weird. The last time Caleb came to see me in the hospital, we'd broken up.

We stood in silence for a beat. Again, I was only alerted to my tears when I felt them on my cheeks. Then, Caleb was right there, wrapping me in his arms. This time, I cried like I hadn't cried in years. Burying my face in his chest, I threw my arms around his waist and hung on. This was about so much more than my stupid roll into a ditch. It was years of missing him and wishing I could fix everything I'd messed up before. It was all of that and the fact I finally felt safe for the first time in what felt like way too long.

He simply held me, one hand tangled in my damp hair and the other circling on my back. He murmured soothing sounds and didn't stop to ask what was wrong or anything. Thank God because I didn't think I could handle that. Not just yet.

After I didn't know how long, I slowly pulled my face away from his chest and looked up. "I got your shirt wet," I mumbled.

Caleb glanced down at me, the corner of his mouth curling up and sending my belly into a few somersaults. "Pretty sure it was already wet."

We stared at each other, my mind a collision of thoughts

and muddled emotions. I'd missed Caleb so damn much for so damn long, I ached to be close to him. Yet, I'd told myself for years I didn't deserve him, and I could hardly contemplate the fact he was here. After a beat, his gaze sobered. "You okay?"

I shook my head, but I couldn't seem to speak.

His eyes widened in alarm. "Let me go get the nurse."

He started to pull away, but I tightened my arms on his waist, shaking my head again. "It's not that. It's just been a shitty day..."

I forced myself to stop talking. I didn't need Caleb, of all people, to know how much I'd stumbled in life. I'd already sent his life careening sideways once before.

"What is it?" he asked, his eyes searing into me. "If you need anything, you know all you have to do is ask."

I almost burst into tears again. Because that was *so* Caleb—he was just a solid guy with a heart of gold and I'd fucked it all up. Everything about him and who he was felt so much bigger in this moment. I'd come running home because I was finally trying to face the mess I'd left behind. A big part of that mess was Caleb and wanting to make things right. Maybe if he could forgive me, I could forgive myself.

"Nothing. There's nothing you can do. I'm just so glad you're here," I said. I meant it so sincerely, it made my heart hurt.

He loosened his hand in my hair and brushed a few locks away from my forehead, checking the bandage there. The cut was right along my hairline, so I was hoping the scar wouldn't be too bad.

"Tell me what's wrong," he said, his tone so careful I almost cried all over again.

I wanted to tell him, but I couldn't. It was too embarrassing.

We stared at each other again. Oh God. It felt so good to be close to him. For the first time in years, I felt like I could relax. I wanted to wrap myself in Caleb and stay there forever.

My next words startled me. "I miss you." The moment those words escaped, I wanted to grab them and stuff them back inside. I didn't need to blurt out all kinds of crazy, emotional stuff. This wasn't supposed to happen this way.

Caleb stared at me, the hand circling on my back finally pausing. He swallowed, the sound audible in the room. My awareness of him was so heightened, the hair on the back of my neck stood up. "You have no idea how much I've missed you," he nearly growled.

Emotion was rushing through me, mingling with desire that should've seemed out of place given everything that had happened, but it didn't. Wanting Caleb came as easily as breathing to me. It always had. I'd forgotten how powerful the draw was. Raw joy rose through the scrum of tattered regret and lingering pain, striking against that desire like flint to stone.

This was me, this was Caleb. Us. There had never been anyone but him in my heart, and my body knew it. He strummed every chord of my being simply by existing in space and time near me.

With a muttered imprecation, he dipped his head, kissing one corner of my mouth and then the other. Oh geez. I was a sucker for corner kisses, at least when it came to him. Two more kisses dusted at the corners of my mouth and then I sighed. His tongue swiped along the seam of my lips, and I let go with a low moan.

I held onto him as if he was a life raft in the middle of the ocean, burrowing into him as our tongues tangled. My heart was beating so fast, I could barely breathe. A pager call came over the hospital speakers, and he drew back slowly, his forehead falling to mine.

We stood like that, our breath coming in heaves. Placing my palm on his chest, I felt his heartbeat racing madly just like mine.

Chapter Three

CALEB

The flames licked high into the sky. I stood at a distance, watching the house in front of the crew burn down. The fire was quickening. We could hear the air starting to rush into it, filling in the spaces opened up by sections of roof collapsing inward. Watching the flames flash high in the sky, my mind spun back over ten years ago.

We were in high school, returning from a fun day of skiing. Ella was with me, along with my best buddy Jake and his girl Holly. Jake and I were seniors, while Ella and Holly were two years behind us in school. It wasn't too late that night, but it was winter in Alaska, so it was dark even at eight o'clock at night. Ella was driving along Turnagain Arm. The name was so accurate, it could almost be a joke. Turnagain Arm was a stretch of highway south of Anchorage. It wound along the shoreline of Cook Inlet, hugging the mountainside. As such, it turned again and again and again, weaving along the inlet to the south and Kenai Peninsula.

On that cold winter night, rounding one of the corners, another car was coming around from the other side. We would later learn the driver was drunk. He plowed into Ella's parents' car, sending the car into a tailspin. It rolled a few times before coming to a stop at the base of a small bluff.

I remembered the smell of fuel and the adrenaline pumping through me. Jake was thrown from the vehicle. Ella and Holly were alive, yet injured. I happened to be in the passenger seat, the only part of the car that hadn't gotten bashed in as it rolled down the bluff.

Back in high school, I'd already started my volunteer fire department training. So I had some idea of what to do. I scrambled out of the car, ignoring the gash on my shoulder. Holly was right behind me. Although she was injured, she crawled through the broken window on the back passenger side. Meanwhile, the smell of fuel was overpowering. In a flash, flames engulfed the car. All I could remember was I needed to get Ella out as fast as possible. She'd gone from crying to deadly quiet. I couldn't hear a thing with the sound of the fire taking hold and roaring in my ears.

I remembered the heat surrounding me as I reached through the flames. By pure luck, Ella was easy to reach, and I dragged her out of the car. We both got burned. She was in much worse shape than me with a ragged gash on her thigh and burns on her side and one of her legs. My forearms were singed, but nothing more. I still had the scars to prove it.

Not that I needed a damn thing to remind me of that night.

After that, I remembered the cold air against my skin feeling strange, and the panic pounding through me as I checked on Ella and raced over to check on Jake. He was dead. He'd been thrown against the rocks near the highway. They told us later he died on impact.

I never forgot the raw fear that raced through me when I saw him—lying limp against the rocks, a deep gash on his forehead, and his neck at an odd angle. Through my fear, I managed to check for a pulse and got nothing. Thinking back, I probably knew he was dead before I even got to him, but adrenaline was pumping through me like crazy. Even without feeling a pulse, I'd attempted CPR—a futile endeavor, but I'd felt like I had to try.

Holly had a few cuts and bruises and a broken arm, but nothing more. She'd been strangely calm, or so it had seemed. She'd stayed at Ella's side while I crossed the highway to check on Jake. Though I supposed I had seemed calm as well. When you're numb with fear and shock, it can look like calm on the outside.

After the accident, I graduated from high school, barely getting through the last few months. The ache of losing Jake and the trauma of how it happened was brutal.

Ella and I broke up. I couldn't tell you now if either one of us wanted that to happen, but it was what happened. She felt responsible for the accident, even though it wasn't her fault. Not at all. She just happened to be the one in the driver's seat when that idiot plowed into us.

So there was that. I went to college, while Ella stayed behind to finish high school and later went to college. The paths of our lives went in different directions. I was drawn back to Willow Brook, my commitment to firefighting only growing deeper as a result of the tragedy. While I hadn't been able to save Jake that night—hell, I hadn't even had a chance—I'd saved many other lives since then.

Except for the other day, the last time I'd seen Ella had been about five years ago. We ran into each other in the grocery store. My mother had been with me, so we'd had a polite interaction and nothing more. It had hurt to see her, if only because she seemed so far away—an edge to her and a distance that had never been there before. When you fall in love, or lust, in high school, well, it's hard to make sense of any of it.

When you were young, everything felt new and powerful—golden days filled with the vitality of youth, the sense that life could give you the chances you wanted. There was that and the blunt fact that youthful lust was like no other—a wild, unrestrained force with no artifice to ruin it. Ella had been quiet, brainy and beautiful. I'd loved everything about her.

Another five years went by. I saw Cade, Ella's older brother, almost every day. He had enough sense to leave me in peace, but then I never knew if he knew how much I missed Ella.

Hell, I didn't know how much I missed Ella until I saw her the other day.

"Caleb!"

I spun around to see the superintendent for my crew calling my name. I walked in his direction, glancing back at the house falling into itself behind me. This call had come in too late for us to keep the house from being destroyed. But we were damn lucky it came in at all. This was a hunting lodge, a nice one. It was surrounded by acres and acres of wilderness. If we hadn't gotten here to control the burn, it likely would've spread and turned into a forest fire.

As it was, we had just returned from a week of dealing with another forest fire about fifty miles north as the crow flies. We were heading into autumn. Fire season was still in full swing here in Alaska.

I reached Ward's side and glanced to him. "Yes?"

Ward flashed a grin. "Thought I'd see if you'd be willing to head back to the station early. We've got this in hand, but there's another fire in town. As you know, Cade's crew is out in the field and the local crew is at training. We're the closest. I figure you take half of our guys and handle that."

"Of course," I replied.

"Perfect," Ward said, his gray eyes narrowing as he watched one of the new guys on our crew knock a ladder over.

I enjoyed working on Ward's crew. He was easy going, once he knew you were solid, that is. I'd taken the position as foreman after Ward's now-fiancée had switched to the local crew because she was having a baby. The timing worked for me. I'd been away from Willow Brook up in Fairbanks for a few years. After I finished my hotshot training, there were no openings here, so I'd taken a position there. When this opened up, I jumped at the chance to move home. I couldn't have guessed Ella would land here.

With a wave, I turned from Ward and gathered up half the crew to go deal with the call.

At the station that evening, I tossed my towel in the hamper after my shower. The fire in town had been fairly minor, which was a good thing because we'd been busy the last few weeks. I slipped onto the bench after changing into fresh jeans and a T-shirt and guzzled a bottle of water. I could hear the television filtering in from the break room, along with the humming sound of a treadmill and feet pounding on it.

Ella was on my brain. But then she'd been on my brain for a week straight now. Aside from when I stopped to see her in the hospital, I hadn't seen her again. Yet. I couldn't stop thinking about her and the way it felt to finally hold her again for the first time in years. Our kiss was seared into my thoughts.

I miss you.

She'd shocked the hell out of me with her words. I hadn't ever quite come to terms with the way things ended with us. In fact, if I were being honest with myself, I knew I'd botched it. I'd missed her ever since.

See, the thing was, we were a mess after that accident. Ella was in the burn recovery center in Anchorage. Holly's injuries had been superficial, but she was a wreck. And Jake was dead. It was so final. My perspective now on death was different, if only because I had faced it enough to understand it was part of life. But back then, Jake's death had hit me hard and left me reeling.

I'd never ever been angry with Ella because I'd known perfectly well she simply happened to be the driver when the other guy ran into us. All of us were struggling with survivor's guilt. Yet, Ella had it the worst. By far. She was also dealing with the most severe injuries. By some miracle, I'd come out of it with nothing more than the burns on my arms and a few other gashes.

When I walked in the hospital that day to see Ella and she'd broken up with me, I reacted in anger because it felt like everything was falling apart then. My best friend was dead, my girl was a mess and she was shutting me out. With steel reinforced doors.

I didn't even know how to describe what seeing her the other day had done to me inside. It had brought back an avalanche of feelings that I'd boxed up and put away. Because I'd felt like I had no other choice. Everything was a knotted mess. If you asked me what was harder—losing Jake or losing Ella—I couldn't have told you because those two losses were all tangled up inside of each other.

To hear that Ella missed me had been like a kick to my gut and a punch to my heart. Then to feel her and kiss her? Hell. It nearly brought me to my knees.

I thought she'd ruined me before, but now it was worse. I knew her, even though I'd tried to forget how well I knew her. Something else was going on. Something or someone hurt her.

With a hard mental shake, I tossed the empty water bottle into the recycling bin in the corner. I stood, snagging my denim jacket out of my locker. I shrugged into it and headed out. I waved at the guys watching television and shouldered through the door into the back parking lot. Cade Masters stood there, talking to his wife—tall, leggy Amelia Masters. With her amber hair and eyes, she was gorgeous, but didn't do a damn thing for me. Which was convenient because Cade would kick my ass.

They'd been married for a few years now. They'd also been high school sweethearts and had a break up for the ages. Despite that, they'd found their way back to each other. I couldn't help but wonder if I could have the same chance with Ella.

Cade said something to Amelia and then slipped his hand in her hair, pulling her close for a quick kiss. She stepped back, her cheeks flushed as she glanced my way. She gave a little wave and then turned, striding to her truck and leaving.

It appeared Cade wanted to talk to me. He waited where he was until I reached him.

"What's up?" I asked, stopping in front of him.

"You seen Ella?" he asked.

I shook my head. "Not since I stopped by to see her in the hospital."

Cade and I hadn't actually spoken about her recent accident and the fact I pulled her out of the car. I figured if he were pissed about it, he would've said something by now.

"I know Beck was worried you took a risk pulling her out by yourself. For what it's worth, I want you to know I would've done the same thing," he said.

My surprise must've shown on my face because he continued. "I heard Beck had words with you about it. I'd never expect anybody to wait around like that. Not that I don't get his point. He's talking rules, but well... Anyway, I think you know what I mean."

"I do," I said simply. "How is she?" My question slipped out unbidden.

Cade eyed me, raking a hand through his shaggy brown curls. There was absolutely nothing feminine about Cade, but Ella and him were so much alike. She shared the same rich brown hair and moss green eyes. Cade was a good guy, and I knew he'd been hit hard by the accident years ago. I'd been too young and too thrown sideways by it to pay much attention to everyone around me, but I remembered him and their parents at the hospital. I knew he worried about Ella, but we'd rarely talked about her.

I sensed Cade had more to say, so I decided to cut to the chase. "Something up with Ella? I mean, aside from her car accident last week."

Cade ran his hand through his hair again, a ragged sigh coming out. "You know Ella does her own thing, and she has for years. You know as well as I do with that accident in high school, well she's never been quite the same. It's not like she hasn't stayed in touch. She has, but she's kept her distance. Something's up though, and I'm not sure what. She had her dream job and now she just up and left. Don't get me wrong, I'm beyond glad she's back home, but... If I sound crazy, all I can say is my gut is giving me a bad feeling. If she trusts anyone, it's you," he said flatly, his eyes locked with mine.

Staring at him, I took a deep breath. I didn't even know how to absorb what he meant. Ella had practically cut me out of her life with a surgical knife after the accident. Why he thought she trusted me was beyond me. "Dude, she hardly talks to me."

Cade nodded. "I know. I'm just saying I know you mean a lot to her. As far as I know, she hasn't dated anyone since high school. Not in any way that was serious."

"Any clue what brought her home?"

Cade shrugged. "I'm not sure, but it's something to do with her job. She left, which doesn't make a damn bit of sense. When she got that job, she wouldn't shut up about how it was her dream. Now, out of nowhere, she quits and comes home."

After a moment, I nodded. "I'll try to talk to her, but I think you're putting more faith in me than you should."

I drove home, turning Cade's words in my mind. My gut told me the same thing with less information than him. With everything Ella had already been through, I hoped against hope it wasn't anything big.

Chapter Four

ELLA

I stood in the parking lot behind Wildlands Lodge, watching my mother drive away after dropping me off. My car had been declared totaled by my insurance company, which wasn't a shocker. The accident hadn't been so bad, but my old hatchback hadn't been worth much. The cost to fix it was more than its value. Sigh. Another thing to deal with.

My mother, of course, insisted on giving me a ride tonight and even offered for me to use her car. I'd demurred on that since Holly had promised me she'd give me a ride home. Much as I didn't like to need anyone, it was nice to be home where I could have some support with those logistical things you miss when you're not near friends and family—a ride to drop your car off at the shop, someone to pick you up from the airport, little things like that. It was hard to quantify how much those things meant until you didn't have them.

There was that and so much more. Caleb being the prime example of *more*. I hadn't realized how deeply I'd missed him. I'd buried it as far down in my heart as I could, so I wouldn't have to think about it.

I spun around and stared out over Swan Lake. Much of my childhood had centered around this lake. The lake was visible in the distance from my parents' house. I used to spend summers along its shores—swimming when it wasn't too cold and mucking about in the tall grasses along its edges. Swan Lake was the centerpiece of Willow Brook. It was a sprawling lake and had lodges scattered around it.

Floatplanes were docked with the setting sun in the distance casting watercolors across everything, pinks and lavenders shimmering on the lake's surface. On the heels of a deep breath, I turned away from the view. My friend Holly, one of my best friends from high school, had called and invited me here to 'grab drinks and catch up' she'd said. As if it was all so simple.

I walked slowly toward Wildlands. Despite the fact that this place was probably the most popular place in town and had been here as long as I could remember, I hadn't spent much time in the bar here at all. If only because as soon as I graduated from high school, I'd left town. The accident that had torn Caleb and I apart had sent me skidding sideways, scooting out of Willow Brook as fast as I could. The grief and guilt had weighed on me so heavily, I had simply wanted to escape and mistakenly thought a change of scenery would give me that. Intellectually, I could tell myself the accident hadn't been my fault, but I'd yet to reach that conclusion inside my heart.

Jake was dead. He'd been Caleb's best friend, Holly's boyfriend, and my friend too. Time had dulled the pain, and I was okay now. *Okay* was about the best I figured I could hope for and maybe even more than I deserved. I didn't do it as often as I once did, but I still replayed the night of the accident in my mind, thinking if only I had reacted more quickly, if only, if only... somehow it would've turned out differently.

I'd moved away as soon as I could, preferring to run from

the painful memories. In running, I'd let other things become too important and that had led me into a mess.

Placing one foot in front of the other, I walked in the back door into Wildlands. Walking down the hallway, I listened to the hum of voices coming from the restaurant and bar. When I stepped into the back of the bar, I glanced around, my eyes searching out Holly. She'd stayed in Willow Brook after high school. She'd gotten her nursing degree and worked in our small hospital here.

Holly waved from over in the corner, her blonde hair standing out in the dim lighting. I couldn't help but smile. Despite all of my mixed feelings, it was good to see her. She'd snagged a booth in the corner. Threading through the tables, I made my way to her.

Before I managed to sit down, Holly stood and engulfed me in a hug. "Oh my god! It's so good to see you," Holly squealed, squeezing my shoulders as she stepped back.

I grinned. She was the same Holly, always bubbly and warm. We'd been a good pair in high school. I was the quieter one with my nose always buried in books, while she was effervescent and funny. Our friendship, born during kindergarten, carried me through the travails of life up until the accident. I had seen her here and there when I visited home while I lived away. After finally accepting I couldn't keep hiding from the painful memories, we'd spent some more time together during my last few visits.

"It's so good to see you," I said as I slipped out of my jacket. Tossing it on the bench seat, I slid into the booth across from her as she returned to her seat.

"What should we order? A pitcher of beer? Or a bottle of wine?" she asked.

I chuckled. "Let's do wine."

Holly grinned. "Wine it is. Alex dropped me off and promised me he'd give us both a ride home later."

Alex was Holly's twin brother and pretty much felt like a brother to me. Though Holly's comment was casual, it came weighted with meaning. The driver who caused our accident and killed Jake had been drunk. I never considered driving if I planned to have a drink, and ditto for Holly and Caleb.

A waitress swung by, taking our order for drinks and then hurrying off after telling us she'd be back in a few minutes with our wine. Holly leaned her elbows on the table, her brown eyes warm and her smile wide.

"Please tell me you're coming home for good. I've missed you," she said.

"I'm planning to stay for now. I'm hoping my position at UAA is a good fit," I replied, referring to the position I'd accepted in the environmental sciences program. In my years of burying myself in my studies, I'd completed a doctorate in environmental science.

Holly, never one to shy away from absolutely anything, got right to the point. "Good. It's about time you come home. No one but you blames you for that accident. Or maybe I should say it in a better way. No one but you blames you for surviving."

Holly knew me too well. We'd had this conversation a few times. Holly didn't understand the depth of guilt I carried. With a sigh, I held her gaze. "Do we have to revisit this? Again?"

Holly's gaze sobered as she nodded emphatically. "Yes. Until you stop feeling bad about it. It. Wasn't. Your. Fault."

Tears pressed hot against my eyes, and emotion clogged my throat. I took a gulp from my water glass, conveniently filled before I'd even arrived. "I know, but maybe..."

"There is no maybe. That guy plowed right into us! There was no way to stop him."

Staring at her, I took a slow breath, wishing my intellect could talk me into this. Because I knew this to be true, but somehow, the guilt clung to me. Jake was dead, and I'd been driving the car. Closing my eyes, I took a steadying breath and met her gaze again. "I know. I'm working on it. Okay? Do we have to stay stuck on it now?"

She reached over and gave my hand a squeeze. "No, we don't. I'm sorry. I just don't like seeing you worry about it for, well, for too damn long. Anyway, what did finally get you to come home?"

"My job went all to hell. So I figured now was the time to come home."

"What the hell happened anyway?" she asked.

I met Holly's gaze and inwardly sighed. If there was anyone I could be honest with, it was her. Despite everything, somehow we'd held our friendship together. I took a sip of water, leaning back when our waitress arrived. She quickly served us our wine, took our food order and then hurried off to the next table. A sip of wine fortified me.

Holly circled her hand in the air, reminding me that our interruption hadn't taken her off track. "It was your dream job, right? What the hell happened?"

My dream job had been a position in the environmental sciences department at the Portland State University. I hadn't considered just how quickly it could get ruined. On the heels of another sip of wine, I eyed Holly. "So there was another researcher on the faculty, Lance Wallace. He worked in a different department, but he was assigned to work on a project with me. Anyway, first he tried to flirt. I ignored it, because I just wasn't interested. Plus, I don't mix work with dating like that. It just gets messy, you know?"

Holly nodded. "Please don't tell me this was a harassment thing."

"He wasn't my boss or anything like that. He got obsessed with me. The only way to describe what he did is stalking. I told our director about it, and she tried to be helpful. But he wasn't doing anything inappropriate at work. It was all the creepy stuff outside of work. He would email me pictures when he saw me having lunch with other guys. Not that they were even dates! No matter how many times I changed my number or my personal email, he'd track me down and send me stuff. It was just relentless. It made me feel crazy, and I finally decided it was best to leave."

Holly's eyes widened, her breath drawing in sharply. "Are you serious?" She paused and took a gulp of wine. "Obviously, I know you're serious. I just can't believe that happened to you. Did you report him to the police?"

"Yeah. They couldn't do much because he wasn't ever physically threatening me..." My words trailed off with a sigh.

Holly took a sip of her wine, her eyes narrowing. "So you just left?"

"Yeah. I thought about everything I would need to do to somehow deal with it, and there were no good options. He had to basically get worse for them to do much. Plus, he'd just made me so miserable. I don't ever want to live anywhere near him. Even though I thought I had my dream job, it wasn't worth it. I got an offer here at the University of Anchorage. It keeps me close to home, and I missed being here anyway. I figure at least here, if anything happens, he won't be able to get away with it. It's too small here."

Holly narrowed her eyes. "Oh hell no. He won't be able to show up around here. Do you think he'd be crazy enough to try to do that?"

"I have no idea. He doesn't know where I am, and I changed my number again. But it's possible he knows where I'm from. It used to be in my bio at the university."

In a way, it was such a relief to tell Holly. I had a few friends in Oregon who knew what was going on, but it wasn't like anyone could stop any of it. Somehow it felt as if this were my karmic payment for the accident that killed Jake. He died, and I got this.

It was also embarrassing. I couldn't fathom how I hadn't seen what was coming ahead of time. I should've been able to pick up on what a creep Lance was. I'd spent far too much time thinking through the minutiae of my early interactions with him to try to assess if I'd unintentionally given him the wrong impression.

"Promise me you'll tell me if you hear from this guy. Because the minute you do, everyone close to you should know about it," she said firmly.

"I promise."

She nodded so emphatically, her hair fell loose from its slapdash ponytail. She snapped the hair band around her wrist and took another sip of wine. "Damn. I can't believe that mess."

I'd been living with it for the last year or more, so the best I could hope for was it might finally be over since I wasn't in the proximity of Lance anymore. I didn't want to dwell on it though. "*Mess* is one way to put it. Anyway, I don't want to get maudlin over it. I'm home and here to stay."

Holly grinned and lifted her glass for a toast. I clinked my glass to hers and took another sip of wine. I needed something to take the edge off tonight. Hell, I needed something to take the edge off of my life. Between leaving my awful cyber-stalker behind in Oregon, getting in a car accident and having Caleb end up being the one to help me, I was topsy-turvy inside.

As I looked across the table at Holly, I caught her eyes angling toward the hallway. Following her gaze, I saw Caleb walking in from the back entrance, his younger brother Nate walking at his side.

The moment my eyes landed on him, he lifted his gaze, his eyes locking with mine from across the room. Barely a free moment had passed when I hadn't thought about seeing him at the hospital and what it felt like to be held in his arms. And those corner kisses—he'd about slayed me with those.

A hum started at my core, swirling in my belly. My pulse gave a funny little jolt. I had meant it when I told him I missed him. Because I had. Everything in my world felt like it was falling in on itself now. The shields I'd built up around my heart were falling away with nothing more than a puff.

I'd only been sixteen years old when the accident happened. I'd been young, full of hope, and madly in love with Caleb. The brutal reality of that accident obliterated my sense of innocence. When I broke up with Caleb, I'd been a mess of confusion, guilt and grief. I'd been in the burn unit in Anchorage, dealing with severe burns on one of my legs and my side. I still had the scars to this day and would forever. To say I'd been a bit of a mess emotionally didn't quite capture it.

Even though I was still grappling with my survivor's guilt, I'd come a long way. Just the fact I'd come home was huge. I might've been running from something, but I was too weary to keep carrying the weight anymore. I'd actually gone to therapy and tried to pull myself together. My therapist had pointedly suggested I try to stop avoiding everyone I'd left behind. I'd gotten pretty pissed off, but her point had been spot on.

Maybe I had some demons to slay and maybe I didn't think I'd ever get past it, but I wanted a chance to start over. Aside from everything else, that was why I'd finally come home.

All along I'd considered my young love with Caleb something I had to leave behind. I knew he'd been bitter when I broke up with him. He lashed out just as I had. We'd both been reeling from Jake's death. I'd figured it was better to leave *us* in the past. In the intervening years, I'd hardly ever been alone with him, if at all. I'd seen him a few times here and there when I came home to visit, but it had always been brief.

One time, I'd known he was seeing someone, and I'd told myself it was for the best. Plans were a funny thing. Since I felt so out of control of my life after the accident, I buried myself in the one thing I could count on—academics. I was a brainy, book nerd all through school. I'd latched onto it to help me get through a lot of pain—emotional and physical. It became my life, with environmental science my love. Growing up in Alaska and watching firsthand how quickly things were changing with the climate had made it a passion of mine. After I graduated from college, I'd been accepted to a doctorate program in Oregon and onto the faculty.

All the while, I'd never stopped missing Alaska, I'd never stopped missing Willow Brook, and I'd never stopped missing Caleb. But I told myself what probably so many people tell themselves—time passed, life changed, and I didn't think I could go back and recapture all that had been lost.

Yet, here I was. I didn't quite know how to bridge the chasm created by time, space, and memory, but I wanted to try.

I didn't realize I was staring until Holly cleared her throat, quite audibly. I felt my cheeks heat as I glanced back to her.

"You know, maybe it's time," she said.

"Time for what?" I asked, forcibly keeping my eyes on her and not looking to see where Caleb and Nate were walking.

"To give Caleb a shot again," she said pointedly. "He doesn't talk about it much, but if you ask me, he never got over you. I know things ended badly. But it was a mess for all of us then, and we were so young to go through that."

"That's one way to put it."

"I still miss Jake," she said softly. "But one thing staying here has done for me is it forced me to deal with it. Bad things happen, and we can still move on."

My heart clenched, and that familiar grief stabbed at me, but I told myself I could handle it now. I reached over and squeezed her hand.

She squeezed mine back and then grinned slyly. "If you're wondering, he's headed right over here. I don't see Caleb as much, but Nate is still best buds with Alex," she said, referring to her twin brother. "So, of course, I see Nate all the time."

Caleb and Nate stopped by our booth. Nate was a few years younger than Caleb and had been in the same grade as Holly and me growing up. Nate shared Caleb's brown hair and eyes and carried himself with an easy-going air. He'd become a bush pilot, flying planes across Alaska's wilderness. With a grin, he glanced to me. "Good to see you home, Ella."

"Good to see you. I can't remember the last time I saw you actually," I replied.

Nate shrugged. "Me neither, but rumor has it you're back to stay."

"For once, the rumors are true."

Caleb's eyes met mine then, and my pulse lunged again, butterflies massing in my belly and heat blooming through me. Sweet hell. I hadn't counted on how much Caleb would affect me. I felt half crazy around him.

"Mind if we join you?" Nate asked.

"Course not," Holly said, sliding over in her seat.

Whether or not they planned it that way, Caleb ended up seated beside me. His familiar scent and the heat of his body were like honey to mine. Having him that close set every cell in my body to humming.

Despite my nerves, being with Caleb, Holly and Nate was so familiar, I felt more relaxed than I had in too long. My old worries fell away and the band of tension around my heart eased. The pain tangled up in our shared pasts didn't seem so awful anymore.

Nate shared a few of his pilot stories and teased Caleb. "Your job's not nearly as stressful as mine," he offered with a wink at the end of a story that involved him landing blind on a gravel runway in the backcountry.

Caleb chuckled, the gruff sound sending a shiver down my spine. "Sure bro. Whatever you say."

"I'd say Holly probably has the most stressful job," I added.

Nate glanced to me. "Why do you say that? She works in the hospital. If she needs anything, she'll be fine."

"Yeah, but she has to deal with every emergency that lands in front of her. At least for you, you can decide not to do something. I mean, you can always decide not to take a trip when the weather's bad." Nate flashed a wry grin before I continued. "And for Caleb, when they're dealing with fires, it's all adrenaline and crazy stuff keeping them going. In the ER, Holly has to try to fix everything and deal with other people freaking out at the same time. Trust me, I bet that's stressful."

Holly grinned and took a sip of her wine, nudging Nate with her elbow. "See, and you think being a pilot is hard."

"Hey, every day, the lives of at least six people at any given point are in my hands," Nate countered with a grin.

Caleb spoke up. "True. A bush pilot in Alaska is considered one of the most dangerous jobs, statistically speaking. That's why mom worries about you."

Nate rolled his eyes. "I'm the baby in the family, and she worries the most about me no matter what. I keep telling her you're the one that runs straight into fires all the time."

Our waitress arrived to check with Caleb and Nate, taking their order and delivering my and Holly's orders.

Holly glanced between the guys. "We're not waiting for your food to come. I'm starving," she said bluntly.

At Nate's eye roll and Caleb's chuckle, we started eating. Their drinks arrived and a few other old friends stopped by the table to say hello as we ate. It felt good to be home. I hadn't had a night like this in years.

While Caleb was waiting for his burger, he stole a few of my fries. It was such a small gesture and something he had done probably hundreds of times when we were dating in high school. Like most teenage boys, he'd pretty much been a bottomless pit when it came to food. Holly was bantering with Nate about a project he was helping her brother with when I glanced up to Caleb just as he bit into one of the fries he'd snagged. It was as if he recognized what he'd done at the same moment I did.

We both froze, staring at each other. My belly did a quick little flip, my tricky heart twisting sweetly in my chest. All of a sudden, emotion knotted in my throat, crashing through me. It wasn't a bad feeling. Rather, it felt so good to have this moment—just a small gesture—I almost didn't know what to do with it. I managed to take a breath, and the tightness in my throat eased.

I smiled because that was all I wanted to do. Caleb flashed a grin and snagged another one of my fries. Within a few moments, their food arrived.

"So Ella, what's the plan?" Nate asked in between bites.

I finished chewing the last bite of my burger and took a sip of my water before glancing to him. "What do you mean?"

"Are you really here to stay? Isn't that like the question of the month?"

Caleb muttered something, but I didn't quite catch what it was. I looked over at Nate and nodded. "I didn't know it was the question of the month, but yes I'm here to stay. I took a position with the University of Anchorage. Most of my time will be handling online classes and research, but I'll go to Anchorage once a week."

I felt Caleb's gaze on me and couldn't resist glancing his way. His rich chocolate brown eyes held mine for a beat, something flickering in their depths. My heart gave another squeeze, and I had to take a deep breath to gather myself.

"Well, that's a damn good thing," Nate said bluntly. "Everyone's missed you."

Nate wasn't known for his subtlety. Holly nudged him again with her elbow. "Of course we all missed her. She knows that."

"Just saying," Nate offered as he chewed a bite of his burger. "I told Caleb…"

"Bro," Caleb interjected, a hint of warning in his tone.

Nate glanced up, a look of innocence on his face. Meanwhile, I wondered about what he meant. The moment passed. I kept drinking wine, while they finished their dinner. Holly's twin brother, Alex, showed up for the agreed upon ride home. Holly glanced to me as she stood, opening her mouth to say something. Caleb spoke before she had a chance. "I'll give Ella a ride home. It's on my way."

I was staying at my parents' house, which was in fact on the way to his parents' house, but I doubted that he was staying there. All I knew was I wanted to snatch those few minutes of time with him.

As Nate stood to let Holly by, she glanced to me, a question in her eyes. "I can hitch a ride with Caleb. Good to see you, Alex," I said, glancing his way and hoping to gloss over any curiosity about my choice.

Alex grinned. "Always good to see you. Holly won't shut up about you being home finally."

In the mix of Nate and Caleb standing, I slipped out of the booth as well. Alex was like a brother to me. He tugged me into a quick hug. Tall and lanky, he shared Holly's blonde hair and brown eyes. "I know I'll be seeing you soon," he offered as he stepped back.

Holly then engulfed me in another hug, whispering in my ear. "You sure you don't need a ride?"

"I'm sure," I murmured.

"Okay, call you tomorrow then," she said as she stepped away. With a wave, she and Alex left.

Nate gave me a quick hug as his name was called over from the pool tables in the back corner. "See you soon," he said with a nod and a wink to Caleb.

Caleb and I were alone by the booth. The hum of voices around us faded as I looked up at him. The moment my eyes met his, electricity pinged through my body, heat blooming from the center outward. I'd forgotten how intent his gaze could be. It was as if I was the only person in the universe to him with his dark gaze searching mine. Without a word, he nudged his head to the backdoor and turned, waiting for me to walk ahead. At the last minute, he tugged his wallet out and tossed cash on the table.

I threaded my way through the tables, feeling Caleb's presence behind me. I was the slightest bit tipsy, but not too much. Though I'd enjoyed my wine, Caleb had nothing more than water. Walking out into the chilly fall evening, I paused as the door fell shut behind us.

"I don't know what you drive," I said, glancing to him as he stopped at my side.

We stood there in the fading light of dusk. A cool breeze gusted across the parking lot, fluttering the leaves on the trees along the lake's shores. A few leaves blew loose, little flecks of yellow in the gloaming.

Time felt as if it was collapsing into itself. I felt as if my past was barreling towards me and flying behind me at the same time. Because, you see, everything with Caleb felt so familiar. Being home felt so familiar. The distinct screech of an eagle cut through the quiet, rising above the distant hum of voices filtering out from Wildlands.

The sound snapped the moment. My belly fluttered and liquid heat slid through my veins. I looked over at Caleb. With his familiar dark brown gaze on me, it felt as if he could see right through me. Without a word, he turned and I followed along at his side, our footsteps crunching on the gravel.

We stopped beside a black truck. As soon as I saw it, I recognized it more clearly from the day I'd seen it. Sometimes I wondered if I felt so safe with him because, by chance or fate or coincidence, he happened to have rescued me twice in my life. Yet, I sensed there was more to it than that. Trust didn't come easily to me, not anymore.

Being cyber-stalked had done funny things to me. It made me question everything—my judgment, my sanity, and always my safety. Yet, with Caleb, that jumpy feeling inside went away. It was an immense relief.

I stopped beside his truck on the passenger side. Turning, I looked up to find his gaze waiting. I'd forgotten how handsome he was. It wasn't as if I hadn't seen him at all. In the ten years since the accident, I'd seen him a handful of times. The last time had been about five years ago—just another passing interaction in town when I was visiting. Each time it hurt to see him, and then I would shove the feeling down, tucking it away so I didn't have to face it.

Yet, here and now, I again experienced that sense of time collapsing. As he stared at me in the wispy light, my heart started to pound hard and deep, sensation spiraling inside. He took a step, and then he was right in front of me. My hips bumped against his truck. My breath hitched and heat flashed through my body.

He lifted a hand, brushing a loose lock of hair off my cheek, his fingers trailing over the stitches at my hairline. "It looks like it's healing okay," he said, his voice gruff.

My voice came out husky. "It doesn't hurt. I have an appointment in another few days to get the stitches out."

He tucked my hair behind my ear, the brush of his calloused fingertips against the sensitive shell sending a hot shiver through me with goose bumps chasing in its wake.

"What did you mean when you said you missed me?" he asked, referring to my abrupt declaration in the hospital last week.

I could hardly hear over the heartbeat pounding through my body. I was a jumble of emotion and sensation. On the heels of a shallow breath, I swallowed. "Just that."

"Why did you come home?"

I stared at him, not wanting to explain everything. Certainly not now.

I didn't even know where to start. How did I explain that I was finally trying to come to terms with what I'd been running from? I was so weary of the muddled guilt about the accident. I felt so awful that Jake had died when I'd been driving and somehow should've, could've been able to stop it from happening. Yet, I needed, no wanted, to lay that to rest if I could. There was that and the fact that what had finally pushed me to come home was a stalker. Dear God. My life was a colossal mess. I gave myself a shake, trying to focus.

Caleb looked through me, his gaze slicing right to my core, to the part of me that had come to doubt so much about myself in the last few years. I pushed back against the feeling. With a hard shake inside, I took a deep breath and told only half the truth. "I missed being here. It was time to come home."

His eyes narrowed, darkening as he searched my face. His fingers sifted through my hair. "And that's all?"

I shrugged. I didn't want to keep talking about this, not right now. Because the truth would come out, yet it was only part of the story. Yes, certain events had pushed me in this direction, yet my desire to come home had been the call in my heart that never died. I didn't like how it felt to consider the rest—how small and vulnerable it made me feel.

Instead, I focused on something else—the heat coiling in my belly and the threads stitching me closer to him. Sliding my hand around the nape of his neck and into his hair, I pulled him down for a kiss.

If he meant to push the point with me, he let it go. Our kiss was a shock of contact, a bolt of lightning through me. It sent white-hot heat straight up my spine and spiraling outward. On the heels of my gasp, his tongue swept into my mouth, and I blessedly forgot everything else.

Chapter Five

CALEB

I told myself I wasn't going to kiss Ella. I told myself there was something else going on with her, and I needed to know. I told myself we needed to untangle the messy emotions left over from the accident. I told myself a lot of things.

Yet, my body trumped my mind. With Ella's body flush against mine as she rose up on her tiptoes and slid her hand into my hair, my brain simply stopped functioning. The moment her lips met mine, that was it. I couldn't resist the sweet heat of her lips, the glide of her tongue against mine.

I didn't know what first love was like for everyone, but I knew what it was like for me. Innocence didn't quite capture it. When it came to Ella and me, there had been an elemental rawness to it, a purity. Everything was light and heavy at once. There were so many firsts that could never be repeated. So much meaning was carved into how I felt about her. There was that and then how things blew apart. Reality had crashed into us, leaving us behind in emotional disarray.

I'd wondered if we could recapture any of it because of how guarded she was now. But it melted away the moment we touched. She'd always been bold with a hint of wildness to her. Just as she was now. Her hand curled into my hair. On the heels of another gasp from her, I crowded against her, my hand gripping her hair almost roughly.

My need for her had been pushed down, forced into hibernation for too many years. No one else had ever quite measured up to it. I'd had a few semi-serious relationships, but they always petered out. Because I kept searching. Searching for something that came even remotely close to what it felt like when I was with Ella.

For a while, I convinced myself it was because of how things ended with us—at a time when we were both a mess and vulnerable for reasons that had nothing to do with our young relationship. And yet, they were tangled up in everything, including the end. Spiraling in my own grief of losing my best friend and worried about her, I could hardly think straight. I'd lashed out when she pushed me away.

And then felt nothing but years of regret afterwards. It had been so obvious she believed—for no logical reason— she somehow could have changed the outcome of that accident. We'd all been hurting, but she'd shouldered an extra burden, and I hadn't known how to help her. I was too young then to navigate the emotionally tricky terrain.

The moment I'd held her again in the hospital last week, I'd remembered everything I'd missed. Now with her kissing me, our mouth's fused together as if we were one, I couldn't get enough.

My hand slid through her hair, down her spine, and cupped her lush bottom. Her perfect, heart shaped ass had starred in a few too many of my fantasies. She groaned as her hips flexed into me. I was rock hard and ready and had been at half-mast since I'd gotten close to her tonight.

I drew back, murmuring her name roughly, my lips blazing a hot trail down her neck, savoring every pant and whimper coming from her. A door slamming in the distance snapped me out of my lust-induced trance. I realized we were in the parking lot in full view of anyone coming in and out of the back of Wildlands. I couldn't bring myself to draw away too far, so I stayed where I was. Pressed against her, I could feel her heart pounding against my chest, its beat as wild as that of mine.

Opening my eyes, I looked into hers, that rich green with tiny flecks of gold. Her lips were puffy from our kiss, her eyes dark. The air was heavy around us, alive and weighted with need and emotion.

"Come home with me," I murmured.

Ella stared at me, her gaze hazy, but sharpening as we looked at each other. "I don't know if that's a good idea," she finally said.

"Tell me why it's a bad idea."

A little laugh escaped, her eyes widening slightly.

"Are you seeing someone?" I asked.

She shook her head sharply, a hint of bitterness flashing in her gaze.

I filed that away, knowing that there was more to every story with her.

"What about you?" she asked in return.

I shook my head. "No."

We stared at each other, the air humming. I desperately wanted her to come home with me, but I sensed I'd be pushing too far and too fast for now. Yet, it didn't change what I wanted.

"I want to say yes," she finally said before going quiet. Her teeth snagged the corner of her bottom lip as she eyed me. Hope flared in my heart, while my body had plenty of its own ideas. "But my parents are expecting me home." Something flickered in her eyes again. Worry, or fear. I wasn't sure what. "Maybe we shouldn't rush."

There were all kinds of things I wanted to say, but I knew none of them were sensible. If there was one thing I didn't want to do again, it was to put my heart out there only to have Ella stomp on it.

For all I knew, she was coming home on the heels of a

break up and I was a potential rebound. So I stepped away from her, though it took an act of pure discipline to do so.

As I started driving towards her parents' place, it occurred to me that the last time I'd actually been in a car with Ella had been the night of the accident. That recognition was a hard kick to my chest. It felt so familiar to be with her.

Chapter Six

ELLA

Walking into the kitchen at my parents' house, I found my mother making breakfast and coffee. Georgia Masters, the town librarian, was a force to be reckoned with. She was a no nonsense and endlessly supportive mother.

Before I'd even spoken, she glanced over her shoulder. "Have a seat dear. I'll get you some coffee and eggs."

"Mom, I can manage to get my own coffee, and you don't have to cook me breakfast every day."

I'd been here just over a week now, and she'd made breakfast for me every day. Not that I minded. My mother was an amazing cook, and it was wonderful, absolutely wonderful, to be home and have her fuss over me.

She set the spatula down on the counter, her green eyes crinkling at the corners with her smile. With her once-brown hair now completely silver, her green eyes stood out more brightly. "I know I don't have to. This is the first time you've been home for more than a visit for years, and I want to spoil you," she said pointedly.

She turned the burner off under the scrambled eggs and pointed to the table. "Sit."

Returning her smile, I walked faster, scooting past her. "I'm getting my own coffee."

Pouring myself a cup of coffee, I added a dash of cream before sitting down at the table. I took a few sips as I looked out the kitchen window. My parents' had a sprawling log home with cottonwood trees scattered around it. This area of Alaska was rocky and hilly in the distant foothills of Denali, the tallest mountain peak in North America and the centerpiece of the Alaska Range. The kitchen looked out over a grassy field with a river running through it. Though I'd never stopped missing Alaska, being here drove the point home. The edge of wildness, the spectacular beauty—it was home to me.

I savored my coffee as I soaked in the view and the feeling of being back here. Within a few minutes, my mother was joining me at the table, serving us both plates of scrambled eggs with feta and red peppers. They were, of course, delicious.

One of the things that had added to my shame about what happened with Lance was I felt like I should've seen it coming. Even when I first met him, he gave me a bad feeling, yet I figured there couldn't be much to it. My mother was such a strong, smart, independent woman. I felt as if I hadn't lived up to the woman I could be.

Shame was a funny thing. It rattled around in your brain, running laps around rational thoughts and winning every race. In that sense, shame was close friends with guilt. Both feelings functioned similarly in how they could take hold in your mind. I recalled talking about my guilt with my therapist after Jake died. My therapist talked about how you just have to accept that bad things simply happen sometimes, even when no one's done anything wrong. She tried to help me walk through to the point where I believed that about the accident. Over and over she walked me through who was actually responsible. Eventually, I'd made it to the point where I could see the possibility of letting go of my guilt. Coming home was the last step, or so I hoped.

The accident was so much messier and sad and heartbreaking and final. It was a single event, yet it sprawled ugly and messy in my heart and mind. When Lance started stalking me, even that led back to the accident. Intellectually, I told myself it made no sense, but a part of me believed I simply didn't deserve happiness and Lance terrifying me the way he did was simply part of the hand I'd been dealt as a result.

Being stalked made me feel crazy. Lance wasn't part of my life in any personal way. Yet, from a distance, he managed to terrify me, to make me look over my shoulder everywhere I went without ever laying a finger on me.

I took a gulp of my coffee, pondering when and how to talk to my mother or anyone in my family about it. As if she could read my mind, my mother glanced up, her way too perceptive gaze coasting over my face. She finished a bite of her eggs. After a sip of coffee, she angled her head to the side. "Your friend Susan called me."

Fuck. Susan was my only friend from Oregon who knew everything that had gone on. She happened to be there one time when I had another bouquet of flowers show up at my apartment—another unwanted bouquet that I promptly stuffed in the trash bin outside, only to find an email the next morning berating me for not appreciating a small gift.

Big girl panties. The only person you need to face now is your mother.

As much as I judged myself, I had faith she wouldn't judge me.

"What did Susan say?"

"Well, she told me what's been going on with that man. Why didn't you say something? Is that why you came home?" my mother asked softly.

My chest felt tight, and my gut started churning. All of

the comfort I'd soaked up during the last week of being here disappeared instantly.

"I wanted to come home anyway," I finally said. "Everything going on with Lance pushed me to make a decision. I'm just hoping now that I'm not working at the same place, he'll forget about me. I don't have much hope he can't track me down. My bio from work used to have my background listed."

I didn't know how much Susan had told her, but since Susan knew it all, I was guessing my mother did too. My mother was quiet, her eyes narrowing.

"Mom, I'm sorry..."

"Oh hon, you don't need to apologize for anything. I'm angry at whoever the hell did this. Susan told me he's been harassing you online for over a year, is that right?" At my nod, she continued, "I'm going to talk to your father tonight and find out what we can do."

My father was the chief of police here in Willow Brook. He always wanted to make everything right. Yet again, my parents would be sweeping in to help me, just like after the accident. It felt like whenever I tried to take control of my own life, something happened that wrenched it out of my control.

After the accident in high school, my family rallied around me, helping me with my recovery, spending days and nights in the hospital afterwards. Caleb had now pulled me out of two car accidents. I was trying to rescue myself for once.

"Isn't this why you wanted to come home? Because you would be safe here, and you wouldn't be alone."

I fought to keep from crying, but tears rolled down my cheeks anyway. "I wanted to come home because I missed it. I'm so tired of ending up in situations where other people have to take care of me. I was handling it. I'm still handling it. If you tell Dad, he's gonna..."

My mother shook her head sharply. "That's what people

do. They help each other. Would you blame a friend if this were happening to them? That's half of strength—asking for help when you need it. I'm not keeping this a secret from your father, so don't ask me to," my mother said flatly.

"And that means Cade will find out and everyone," I muttered, referring to my older brother. Who I adored by the way, but he didn't need to worry about me either.

My mother took a deep breath, pausing to take a sip of coffee and then lasering me with her gaze. "Your brother loves you. I wish you had said something sooner. I can't believe this has been going on for over a year."

I wanted to stomp my feet, but I was also relieved. Because she was right. I'd been stubbornly trying to deal with this on my own, and I couldn't. I looked over at her, knuckling my tears away. "I know," I finally said. "I just kept thinking it would somehow stop."

My mother stared at me quietly, her gaze becoming steely. "People like that don't stop until they're made to stop."

The tension balled in my chest and heart for so long started to ease slightly. "Fine. I know you'll want to talk to Dad, and I'll deal with it. If you can wait, I'll tell him myself."

My mother reached across the table and squeezed my hand quickly. "Thank you."

We ate quietly for a few moments before she spoke again. "How about you tell me about your new job? Or better yet, I noticed Caleb gave you a ride home last night."

I felt my cheeks heat, but ignored it. "Mom, it was just a ride home."

I elected not to fill her in on the fact that he'd kissed me senseless and nearly melted me in the parking lot behind Wildlands. She'd probably be ecstatic. But I wasn't ready to go there. Not just yet.

"So, my job. As you know, I accepted a position on the faculty at UAA in the environmental studies department. I'll be teaching a few courses every semester in their hybrid program, which is a combination of online classes and on campus. I'll go to Anchorage once a week, but otherwise I'll be able to work here. It works out perfect for me. I figure one trip to Anchorage every week will be easy. If you need me to do any shopping, I'm your girl. I just need to find a place to stay soon."

My mother's features tensed. "I'd rather you just stay here for now. At least then, you're not alone."

I met my mother's steely gaze. For a moment, I wanted to argue the point. Because I was sick of what Lance had put me through. Though he'd never approached me outside of work, I'd hated being alone when I'd randomly receive emails or texts from him.

I finally shook my head and sighed. "Let's just see what happens, Mom. I won't do anything stupid. I'm hoping now that I'm gone, it'll be out of sight, out of mind for him."

I took another sip of my coffee and stood from the table. "I need to get ready to head into Anchorage for the day."

My mother nodded, standing with me before I had a chance to turn away. She pulled me close for a hug, squeezing me tight. My mom was a big hugger, every hug gave me a chance to absorb her strength for a moment. I stepped back, feeling stronger than I had in a long time.

"What are you doing today?" I asked.

"Going to the library, of course," she offered with a smile.

———

Later that day, I walked down the hallway at the university. I'd met a few of my colleagues, and so far, everyone was quite nice. It felt good to be somewhere new, where I could focus on my research and teaching and not worry about someone watching my every move.

While I didn't have an office here because it wasn't necessary, there was a swing space that was used by a number of faculty members who worked from a distance as I would. There were faculty members from all over the state. Geographically speaking, Alaska was a sprawling state, by far the largest in the country. It was a fifth the size of the entire United States. Yet, it felt small in other ways. When you lived in a place as remote as this, bonds built quickly. Everyone made sacrifices to be here. The love of the land and its spectacular beauty and wildlife made it all worthwhile.

As I drove back from Anchorage, I felt the ball of tension that had been held tightly somewhere between my heart and my belly start to loosen slightly. It felt so damn good to be home. The drive from Anchorage to Willow Brook was gorgeous.

Vistas of the mountains were in one direction with the ocean on the other as the highway rolled through the wilderness. Autumn in Alaska was lovely, a kaleidoscope of oranges, yellows and reds. Unlike some parts of the country, Alaska didn't have as many hardwood trees with so many evergreens covering the state. Clusters of birch and cottonwood turned yellow and orange in this part of the state. The wild variety of bushes created an explosion of color low to the ground, rich reds and purples dancing under your feet. The hills rolling in front of me offered bursts of color in between the trees.

As I approached Willow Brook, I spied a cluster of moose nibbling on alder trees beside a field. Though it was early autumn, there was a sense of quickening in the air with the days getting shorter so fast. People who weren't from Alaska often asked if the winters were miserable here because it was long, dark and cold. I would never argue that I loved those dark months, but there was a peaceful quality to them. Autumn felt alive, that last burst of energy before we settled into the quiet of winter when the days were shorter and the nights longer.

Before I reached Willow Brook, I turned off the highway

into a viewing spot. Climbing out of the car, I walked over and leaned against the railing. This particular spot offered a view of a lake on the outskirts of Willow Brook, nestled in a valley between the mountains. A few trumpeter swans floated serenely on the surface with the sun casting a pink glow over them as it slipped down the sky.

I breathed in deeply, smelling a hint of wood smoke in the distance. When I climbed back into the car, I felt my phone vibrate in my pocket. Pulling it out, I glanced down to see a text from Caleb. Just seeing his name had my pulse quickening. I wanted to see him so badly. I wondered what he would think of my years away. I'd tried to run and let the wildness take over at first, partying a bit too much, flirting a bit too much, yet never letting things go any further because it just didn't feel right. I'd tried to chase the pain away, only to find that that wasn't possible. It was only when I faced it that it eased.

Meet me for dinner?

I stared at his text, my thumbs hovering over the screen. While I was busy telling myself I should wait to reply, my thumbs were ahead of me.

Sure. Where?

Firewood Café. Quieter than Wildlands.

Ok. What time?

I can be there in 10.

I'm about 20 minutes away.

See you in 20.

Staring at my phone, I contemplated what I wanted. Actually, I didn't have to contemplate what I wanted. I needed to contemplate what I was going to do about what I wanted. I wanted to have it all—to get back what was taken from us in an ugly accident. I wanted to lose myself in Caleb because I sensed he could give me the escape that I craved. I wanted to get back in touch with myself and to not be afraid and skittish. I wanted to not feel like an object. Oddly, even though Lance never once touched me, the way he stalked me online had made me feel like nothing other than an object. I hated the feeling.

With Caleb, I felt nothing but real. All the pain I'd tried to escape anchored me in the depth of emotion running between us.

As I started my car, I considered that I was currently staying with my parents. While I was an adult, it was a courtesy to let them know my plans. I knew I was *not* going home tonight. But that meant a rather awkward phone call. My mother was no prude. "Fuck it," I muttered to myself.

I contemplated texting her, but I knew that would lead to nothing but questions. As I pulled out of the viewing spot, I called her, tapping on my speakerphone in the car.

She answered on the first ring. "Yes dear?"

"Hey Mom. I'm calling to let you know I won't be home tonight."

"Oh, ooo-kaayyy," she said slowly.

"I'll be with Caleb," I explained, deciding to cut straight to the point.

I prayed she didn't ask more questions. If I ended up coming home, that would be fine too.

I could hear the smile in her voice when she replied. "Okay dear. I'll just let your father know you're with friends."

"Mom, you know I'm twenty-six years old, right?"

"Obviously I know how old you are dear. I'm the one who gave birth to you," she said with a chuckle. "I appreciate you had the courtesy to let me know, especially after our conversation this morning. But it's not like your father won't wonder where you are, so I have to say something. Although truth be told, he'd be thrilled to know about you and Caleb. You know my feelings on that," she said pointedly.

I swallowed my sigh. "I do, Mom. Can I get off the phone now?"

Another soft laugh from my mother. "I appreciate your call. Real quick though, can I ask you one more thing?"

"Sure."

"Are you okay with it if I talk with your father tonight about our conversation this morning?"

God, I loved my mother. I knew it would probably kill her to sit on this, but she wouldn't say anything if I asked her to wait. "It's fine, Mom. I'm sure he'll want to talk to me about it, but there's time for that later."

Her sigh was audible. "Thank you dear. Tell Caleb I said hello."

"Geez Mom. You tell him the next time you see him. Which I'm sure will be any day now."

At her laugh, we said goodbye. With my pulse quickening and anticipation searing through my veins, the rest of the drive to Willow Brook felt endless.

Chapter Seven

CALEB

There was an edginess to Ella, a restless, heightened quality. Looking at her across the table, all I could think was it was so damn good to have her back home. We were just finishing dinner, and it had been the longest period of uninterrupted time I'd had with her since I could recall. Her brown hair fell in a tousle around her shoulders. Her cheeks were flushed slightly, the green of her eyes standing out. I could've looked at her for hours, if only because for the first time in way too damn long I had the opportunity to do so. Maybe, just maybe, we'd get a chance to write a different ending for ourselves this time.

I wasn't kidding myself. In between the time since I saw her at the hospital after her minor car accident and then again the other night, I'd shifted gears inside. After ten years of telling myself I had no choice but to let go and move on, she was here. Back to stay. I was under no illusions that things would be simple. Yet, I thought maybe we had a shot.

Everything about Ella was colored by more than one lens for me. First, there was the fact that she'd been my high school love. Let's face it, young guys aren't exactly known for their brilliance in high school. Especially not when it came to matters related to girls. I doubted any man would argue that his cock was a brilliant decision maker.

I'd have been lying through my teeth if I said my initial attraction to Ella had been about anything other than lust. I'd started out *in lust* with her and then fallen *in love* with her. I had enough sense to know that phase of my life was what it was. Then, there was the tangled mess of the accident. The accident that had been no one's fault except for the man who'd been drunk and driving recklessly down the road. For the four of us in that car, his reckless decision had left Jake dead and scars—literal and metaphorical—in its wake.

I'd been so angry with Ella when she broke up with me, too hurt to see through to the other side of it. Reeling already, to have her shut me out had been like a slice to my heart. Even worse, I'd been worried sick about her. She was in the hospital for weeks, which felt like forever at the time. If you'd asked me to explain why I was angry, I couldn't have told you. I supposed I felt abandoned at a time when I needed her and when being there for her was something I needed.

The intervening years had helped me come to terms with Jake's death. Sometimes all you could do was accept that life wasn't fair and that shitty and sometimes tragic things could happen to anyone. I'd also gained some perspective on how Ella must've felt back then. My injuries had been far more minor than hers. She'd been in pain and carried so much more guilt since she'd been driving, if only by chance.

Even though Ella had always been in the back of my mind, I'd mostly convinced myself we'd never have a shot again. Now we did, and I'd be damned if I'd allow it to slip through my fingers.

Janet James, the owner of Firehouse Café, was checking on a couple beside us and then stopped at our table. She snagged an empty chair nearby and sat down. Reaching over, she squeezed Ella's shoulder. "It's so good to have you home. You have no idea how happy I was when Cade told me you were here to stay."

Ella grinned. "It's good to be home and good to see you. How have you been?"

Janet, with her dark hair shot through with silver and her twinkling brown eyes, glanced between us. "I'm fine, busy as ever. Please tell me this means something."

Janet was utterly shameless, and I didn't doubt she had her own opinions about what should be happening between Ella and me. For once, I was on board with her meddling, but I'd follow Ella's lead. I simply shrugged and chuckled. "We're having dinner." Glancing over at Ella, I saw her cheeks pinken slightly. Fuck me. All it took was a flush on her cheeks to send a bolt of lust through me.

By no means were my feelings for Ella purely sexual, but damn she made me fucking crazy. She always had back in high school. I'd loved the contrast of how beautiful she was with her slightly wild edge, and yet she was such a book nerd. Her grades were definitely more important than me back then. She'd been a challenge for me, and I'd loved every minute of it.

Ella met Janet's grin and rolled her eyes. "Just dinner."

Janet smiled as she stood up when her name was called from the kitchen. "I couldn't help but tease. You've been gone too long, so it was overdue."

At that, Janet turned away, replacing the chair she'd borrowed from the other table before quickly collecting our empty plates and hurrying toward the kitchen. Ella watched Janet walk away, her eyes scanning the small café. It looked much the same as it had back when we used to come here after school.

Aptly named Firehouse Café, it was housed in the town's original firehouse from the early part of the twentieth century. The upstairs has been converted into storage. What was once the garage for the fire trucks was now the café.

The concrete floor was stained a soft blue with small round tables scattered around. The fire pole was painted with whimsical fireweed flowers, and local artwork rotated on the walls. The deli counter was to one side with the kitchen behind it. Janet ran this place on her own and had for many years since her husband passed away. The café opened daily at five in the morning for coffee and baked goods and remained opened through lunch and into an early dinner.

Ella's eyes made their way back to me, her cheeks still flushed. "It's still the same," she commented.

I nodded. "How was your dinner?"

"Delicious of course."

Ella had opted for a maple glazed salmon burger, while I had enjoyed a King crab melt, the Alaskan version of a crab melt sandwich.

I wasn't thinking about my words, so what slipped out next surprised me. Although it was the bald truth. "I missed you. I'm glad you're here to stay."

She didn't look away, her cheeks flushing a deeper shade of pink. "I missed you too," she finally said.

"Are you going home after this? To your parents' place?"

She held my gaze for a beat, the air coming to life between us. She shook her head slowly. "I don't think so."

At her answer, my pulse quickened, the need I'd been trying to hold at bay rising inside, crashing against the rocks of my discipline. "Let's go then."

"Let me run to the restroom."

She slipped out of her chair. I watched as she walked across the restaurant, her hips swinging with her steps. She'd filled out since high school, her hips and her breasts more lush. As I waited, all the while telling myself I couldn't just tackle her like a greedy boy, her phone buzzed where it sat in the center of the table. It buzzed again and again and again, one banner after another of texts appearing on the screen. She'd left it face up. My gut pinged. I wasn't even thinking when I spun the phone around.

Did you think I wouldn't find your new phone number?

Did you think you could go back to Alaska and get away from me?

Think again.

I can ruin your career.

Distance doesn't make a difference to me.

You're a fucking whore.

I gave you a chance to give me a chance.

You're such a fucking coward.

Fury coiled inside of me. I didn't know who this was, but whatever was happening was connected to whatever I sensed Ella was hiding. Whoever the hell this was had been making her life miserable, and I would fucking make them pay.

Ella returned to the table before I had a chance to get my anger under control. Her eyes met mine and then flicked to the phone on the table.

"Who is this?" I asked.

Ella sat down quickly, two bright red spots appearing on her cheeks, her eyes widening and fear flashing in them. "It's nothing. It's no one."

"Ella, this isn't nothing. They're threatening you."

Ella stared back at me, her lips tightening into a line and her eyes shuttering. It was similar to the look in her eyes the day we'd broken up when she was still in the hospital after the accident. She had a stubborn streak, especially when she thought she needed help.

I wrestled inside, trying to manage my fury. My anger wasn't with her. It was with whoever the hell was sending her threatening messages. Shackling my frustration, I forced myself to take a deep breath and reached across the table, catching her hand in mine. "Ella, I don't want to fight with you on this. If this has something to do with why you came back, just tell me. Hell, tell your father. At least he could maybe help."

She stared at me, her shoulders rising and falling with a shuddering breath. She didn't tug her hand loose from mine, but gripped it tightly. Running her free hand through her hair, she sifted the glossy brown locks through her fingers. On the heels of another deep breath, she finally spoke, her voice coming out raspy. "This isn't the only reason I came home, but it pushed me to make a decision."

"Who is this?" I asked, pointing at her phone between us, the screen now dark.

"His name is Lance Wallace. He's a researcher at the same university where I was working in Oregon."

"And?"

Her hand fell loose from her hair, thunking on the table. She was still gripping mine, so tightly it was as if she was trying to hold on to me. "He wasn't in my department, but when I started working there, he asked me out. I wasn't interested, so I said no. I didn't think anything of it. He never did anything at work, but..." She paused, spinning a ring on her pinkie in circles with her thumb. "I don't know why, but he was obsessed with me. Somehow he got my personal number and email, and well, this started. I don't know why. You have to understand. I wasn't involved with anyone, not the whole time I was working there. But I have friends and he'd send me pictures of me having lunch with friends and pictures of my apartment. I told my director about it, and she tried to help. But nothing worked. He never physically threatened. Just... stuff like this," she said, gesturing to her phone sitting innocuously between us on the table.

Anger flashed hot inside, but I shoved it away. Right now, Ella was right here, safe with me. "Have you talked to your father?" I asked.

"Not yet. I just told my mother today. She's going to tell him about it. I talked to the cops down there, and it's not like they didn't try to help, but he never made physical threats and he never did anything in person, so there wasn't anything they could do. He just harassed me by text and email. It makes me feel crazy."

The anger inside ran hot and then cold. I wanted to know where the hell this guy was. To make it stop. Yet, I knew Ella didn't need to see how fucking furious I was.

"Mind if I talk to your dad about it?"

Ella's dad was the chief of police for Willow Brook and had been for years. I liked Rex and respected him. He'd been like a father to me in some ways, if only because I'd spent so much time at their house when Ella and I were dating in high school.

"Of course you can talk to him." She looked down, staring at her phone. On the heels of another deep breath, she lifted her eyes. "Do we have to keep talking about this? I know you want to fix it because, well, because you're you," she said with a little laugh. "But it's taken over so much of my life. I don't want it to take over everything here too."

I absolutely wanted to fix this. Now. But she had a point. There wasn't a damn thing I could do right this second, other than support her. If she didn't want to keep talking about it, then we wouldn't. "I only have one question for now," I replied.

At her nod, I asked, "You've already changed your number, right?"

"Several times," she said simply, her gaze weary.

Swallowing my frustration and the helplessness I felt because I wanted to kick this guy's ass, but he wasn't here for me to do that, I let it go. "I'll talk to your dad tomorrow, okay?"

I hadn't seen Ella regularly for a decade, but I knew her very well. I could feel the frustration rolling off of her, the urge to argue the point with me. Yet she didn't. Even though she'd already said it was okay for me to talk with her father, I knew she wouldn't want anyone to interfere. But this wasn't something I was willing to leave alone. Her lips tightened, her eyes narrowed, and then she gave her head a shake. "Fine. Can we talk about something else now?"

Her question was so abrupt with that hint of demanding

and bossy. Despite my frustration, I laughed. "Yes. As long as you promise to let any of us know if this keeps up," I said with a nod towards the poor phone sitting on the table.

Ella rolled her eyes, but she nodded. "As if I could keep it from anyone at this point," she muttered. "Holly knows, my mom knows, you know, and by tomorrow my dad and Cade will know. I figure now that I've left Oregon, he'll eventually drop it."

My gut told me otherwise, but I stayed quiet. There was no need to speculate, not right now. "You ready to go?" I asked.

At that rather opportune moment, Janet stopped by our table, dropping off the check and providing a welcome interruption to shift away from the unpleasant topic. "Good to see you two," she offered, her gaze lingering on Ella. "Promise me you'll be back soon."

Ella smiled, the tension leaving her face. "Of course. You have the best coffee in town. You can bet you'll see me a few times a week."

With a satisfied grin, Janet squeezed her shoulder and whirled away, stopping by the table next to us. I tossed enough cash on the table to cover our bill and the tip before standing, never once letting go of Ella's hand. She glanced to her phone. Actually, glare was more what she did.

"Do you need to use that number?" I asked.

She met my gaze, bitterness flashing in hers. "It gets old changing it, but right now it doesn't really matter anymore."

"Why don't you take my phone? I'll take this one."

Ella's eyes widened, a little laugh escaping. "You want to trade phones?"

"Why not? This isn't my work phone. I have an on-call one for the station. This way, you can just give everybody my number and I'll give this guy hell if he keeps bugging you."

She stared at me for a long moment, a slow smile stretching across her face. After the last few minutes, I was relieved for the tension to dissipate. "Works for me," she said.

I picked up her phone and slipped mine out of my pocket, handing it over. "Passcode?" I asked.

She recited the numbers, and I quickly opened the screen. I was about to enter my number in her contacts, but grinned when I saw it was already there. "Easy to get in touch. You're already in my contacts, so just call you when you want to call me."

I handed my phone to her.

"What's your passcode?" she asked in return.

"Don't have one." I shrugged and caught her hand in mine. "Let's go."

"You sure it's okay I have your phone?" she asked as we started walking out.

"I'm sure."

"You don't have, I don't know, anyone who might want to call you or something..." Her words trailed off.

"If you're asking if I have some ex who would call or anyone I see casually, no. I wouldn't be here with you, and I haven't seen anyone for a while. You don't need to worry about any random texts showing up, or anything like that."

We pushed through the door, the bell jingling behind us as we stepped outside. I paused and glanced to her just as the wind gusted across the parking lot, blowing her hair in a swirl. Her cheeks were flushed. Looking up at me, she bit the corner of her bottom lip, an old habit that never failed to get to me. A bolt of lust hit me at the sight of it.

"I mean, not that it matters if you were," she said.

"It would matter to me," I replied, angling to face her fully.

Looking up at me, she was quiet for a moment, her eyes searching mine. After a moment, she took a breath and nodded.

Turning, I walked toward my truck to find her mother's

car parked right beside it. "Any plans to get a new car?" I asked, pausing at the back of my truck.

"I need to figure that out, but Mom swears it's no problem for me to use this. Dad's been dropping her off at work. I'll figure it out soon. Anyway, I don't know where you live," she said, getting right to the point that mattered.

"Out past Fireweed Lane. Follow me."

Chapter Eight

ELLA

With the wind gusting and leaves skittering across the road and the moon rising above the mountains ahead, I followed Caleb's truck. I knew Willow Brook by heart. Fireweed Lane was a few miles beyond downtown with houses scattered amongst the trees and small lakes in the area.

I was curious to see where Caleb lived. Once upon a time when we were silly teenagers, young and in love, we teased about him building a house for us. He was the kind of man who did just about everything. His father was an engineer and had always been in the middle of some sort of project—from simple construction to elaborate projects. Caleb had been raised to do just about everything. It was fair to say most men in Alaska were the quintessential, rugged handymen. Because when you lived on the edge of the wilderness, it was best to be able to do what you needed on your own.

Though I was vaguely aware of the beautiful view of the moon rising above the mountains amidst the last streaks at sunset staining the sky with violet, I was focused on the taillights of Caleb's truck, as if they would lead me to salvation.

Within a few moments, I was rolling to a stop behind his

truck. Glancing around, I took in the area. The house sat on a gradual slope. Trees were scattered about with spruce and birch mingling. The slope led down to a stream that meandered along the edge of a grassy field. Denali was behind us here with a clear view of the mountains in the distance.

The house was an octagon shape with gray siding and a purple stainless steel roof. Caleb loved his projects, so I shouldn't have been surprised he had a home that wasn't typical. He stepped out of his truck and walked around to meet me. "It's beautiful here. Nice house."

His mouth hitched up at one corner, tugging on the strings of my heart and sending flutters spinning in my belly. "Thanks. I built it myself with my father's help. I got the design from an engineer down in Diamond Creek," he explained, referring to a small town several hours south of Willow Brook. Diamond Creek was a well-known destination, as it was situated on the pristine waters of Kachemak Bay and had a world-class ski lodge.

"Come on in," he said, gesturing toward the house. Following him up the steps onto a curved deck, we stepped through a doorway.

Entering into the kitchen, I glanced around. The space felt open and airy with windows on three sides and a wall at the back with a single door. A counter ran along the wall in the kitchen area with a sink and stove there. An island across from it followed the curve of the wall. There were stools along the counter. The living room was beyond that with a sectional couch and a television mounted on the wall to the back. A fireplace tiled with gorgeous river rocks was in between two of the windows.

The walls were painted a soft gray with a few black-and-white photographs mounted throughout the space. Caleb had loved to take photos in high school, and I recognized one in particular of the moon above Swan Lake. A spiral staircase was tucked in the corner just beyond the door in the back wall.

I glanced to him. "It's beautiful."

"Thanks," he said simply. "You're seeing just about all of it down here." Pointing to the door at the back, he continued. "That's a bathroom and laundry. Come on, I'll take you upstairs."

I followed him up the spiral staircase where we came into another open space. There were bookshelves under the windows here with two chairs facing out toward the view. There were two doors against the back wall leading to a small guestroom and a master bedroom with its own bathroom. The furniture throughout the home was modern and comfortable looking with the wood light and most of the fabric sage green.

In his bedroom, a dresser sat against one wall under the windows with a massive bed to one side. An archway led into a bathroom tiled in sage green with a shower enclosed in glass and a luxurious bathtub. Glancing into the shower, I looked back over my shoulder.

"Well, you won't be saving any water in here," I offered with a laugh, pointing to the multiple jets mounted on the walls.

Caleb was standing over by the door, his shoulder resting against it and one hand in his pocket. His mouth hitched at the corner, his grin sending my belly into a tizzy of flutters.

"It's recycled water. The whole house is run on solar and wind power. I can use a lot of water if I want since I'm not wasting any."

"Really? How'd you work that out?"

"That place in Diamond Creek, Off the Grid, is run by Owen and Ivy Manning. They're environmental engineers, and their specialty is designing places like this."

"I didn't even notice the solar panels on the roof," I said wonderingly.

"They're on the back side. I got a deal on the design by volunteering to let them test different wind collection designs for the house. Right now, if you walk through the trees near the house you'll see a bunch of wind chimes. They're cute, but they're busy collecting energy."

"Oh wow! I've heard of Off the Grid, but I completely forgot they relocated to Alaska."

"I can take you down there to meet them sometime. You'd really like them. Owen's a great guy, and Ivy's brilliant. Maybe as brilliant as you," he said without the slightest bit of sarcasm.

I rolled my eyes, feeling my cheeks heat. "Given what they've accomplished, I'm pretty sure she's more brilliant."

Caleb shrugged. "So you say. Come on downstairs."

For a moment, I wasn't sure I wanted to go back downstairs. In fact, Caleb's bed looked beyond tempting. While I knew just what I wanted, I didn't want to rush. Not any of this.

He'd already turned away and was walking back down the spiral staircase, so I followed. When we reached the kitchen, he opened the fridge and glanced over.

"Wine? Beer?"

I shook my head. I was too keyed up to try to wind down. "No thanks."

At that moment, there was a scratching sound at the door. Stepping away from the refrigerator, he opened the kitchen door. A gigantic cat came dashing through.

The cat was bright orange swirled through with white and close to the size of a small dog. "Hey Creamsicle," Caleb said, leaning down to pet the cat twining around his ankles. He glanced over to me. "This is Creamsicle. Technically, he owns the house."

I laughed as I looked down at the aptly named Creamsicle. "He's huge," I observed.

Caleb straightened after a last stroke over Creamsicle's back. "That he is. He's solid muscle though. He's got the run of the house and all the property nearby. He's tough as hell. An eagle tried to pick him up once, and he fought it off."

Creamsicle ambled over to me with a twirl around my

ankles, his purr audible. Leaning over, I scratched his cheeks and ran my hand over his back as he arched up into my touch. "How did you end up with him? It doesn't seem ideal to have a cat when you're gone a lot the way you are," I said, referring to his job as a hotshot firefighter.

Caleb shrugged. "It's not ideal, but he found me. One day, he showed up on the back porch in the winter, starving and meowing like crazy. I have no idea where he came from. I asked around town, and no one claimed him. My best guess is maybe one of the hunters lost track of him at one of their hunting cabins nearby. I brought him inside that night, fed him, and he's never left. My parents stop by and feed him when I'm out at fires."

Caleb and I stood there, staring at each other for a moment. Creamsicle meandered off to the corner. Finally breaking free of Caleb's gaze, I almost laughed aloud when I realized Caleb actually had a cat bed in the windowsill. After a few sips of water, Creamsicle leapt onto the windowsill, settled into his bed and promptly began cleaning himself.

Caleb turned away, walking to the fireplace and leaning over to start a fire. I was restless and antsy with little jolts of electricity zinging through me in all directions. I hadn't noticed the chill until I heard the sound of the fire taking hold. Walking over to stand beside him, I looked down as the flames flashed amongst the logs and kindling.

He turned to face me, taking a few steps and resting his hips on the back edge of the couch. His eyes caught mine for a beat and then flicked down. The heat of his gaze sent a flush through me, blooming from the inside out.

I tried to remember the last time I'd felt like this. It wasn't as if I'd gone without sex for a decade. Well, I had the last year or more because I'd been freaked out about Lance and his obsession. A few years prior, I had tried to lose myself in anything other than my grief. Yet, nothing took the edge off of it, the wild restlessness lingered and kept me seeking solace in physical escape. Although there had never been any escape. Sex had felt strangely distant.

Caleb was quiet for several taut moments. "Tell me again why you came home," he said, his voice breaking into the quiet.

His question startled me, but I answered almost immediately. "Because I wanted to."

"It's not just because that guy's been making your life a living hell?"

I shook my head sharply, a flash of annoyance rising inside. Not annoyance with Caleb, but with the situation. "I won't pretend he didn't push me to make a decision, but I wouldn't have made it if I didn't want to. Why does it matter?"

It felt as if he was looking straight into the heart of me. The heat of his gaze was so intense, my heart began to pound, every beat echoing through me.

"Because you mean a lot to me," he said, his voice gruff and his eyes darkening. "I won't pretend this is just a fling. Everything between us ended in a mess, and I want a chance to make it right."

"I do too."

My voice came out in a raspy whisper. I felt as if I were a speck in a vast ocean, trying to stay afloat, yet tossed asunder with waves crashing over me. I understood what he meant, and I knew what I wanted. Yet, it terrified me at some level. I took a deep breath in an effort to calm the rushing feeling inside, although it was rather futile. I couldn't tear myself free from his gaze, simply looking at him set me on fire.

Restless, I stepped to him, lifting a hand and tracing my fingertip along his brow, over the slope of his cheek and down along his strong jaw. Touching him anchored me, offering a concrete point of contact amidst the turmoil inside. I didn't feel so lost and wild inside when I was touching him. Since I could hardly bear to think, I wanted to lose myself in him, in sensation.

His breath drew in sharply when I traced my thumb across his bottom lip. For a man, he had lush, full lips. With his dark hair, his chocolate brown eyes, the strong, chiseled features of his face, and his hard, muscled body, nature had been generous with him. To have a mouth like his, sensual and full, on top of everything else didn't seem quite fair.

It felt as if little bolts of lightning were bouncing between us, the air nearly vibrating with intensity. He caught my hand in his.

"Ella. Do you want this?" he asked, the ragged edge to his voice sending a shiver up my spine.

Time was moving like molasses and at the speed of light simultaneously. All the while, sensation built inside. The rush and hum in my body propelled me to impulsively move a step closer, between the cage of his legs and coming against his hard body. The feeling sent a bolt of heat straight through me.

"Yes," I murmured, right before I brought my lips to his.

He was taller than me, but with his hips resting against the back of the couch, we were about level. He held still for a beat when our lips met, and I thought for a minute, he was going to make me wait. Yet, after a moment of stillness, he released my hand and slid one hand into my hair and the other down my spine to cup my bottom. With a growl, his tongue swept into my mouth.

Oh. My. Wow. There was what I wanted and then there was what was happening. I hadn't forgotten the kiss the other night in the parking lot, nor that first point of contact in the hospital. But *this*, this was more than a fleeting interaction. I threw myself into our kiss, my tongue tangling with his, pressing as close as I could to him. I wanted to bury myself in him and wrap his strength around me.

I didn't like thinking about it, but I'd felt so alone for too many years. Right here, right now, I didn't feel alone.

With recklessness spurring me, my hands were greedy—one sliding up under his shirt at the back, savoring the flex of his muscles, while the other mapped the planes of his chest. He was stronger now—all of him so much more of a man than he'd been before. When you're young, eighteen seems like a man, but the ten years that had passed had built him into so much more physically. He worked one of the most physically demanding jobs in the world with the hard planes of his body showing it. He broke free from our kiss, leaning back as his hand slid from my hair to cup my cheek. One look in his eyes unleashed a mass of butterflies in my belly.

"I missed you. So fucking much."

At Caleb's words, emotion hit me, so hard I almost lost my breath. All the loneliness, all the grief, all the *everything* I had stuffed away inside rose, clamoring to be free. Tears pricked hot at the backs of my eyes. I could hardly catch my breath as I stared at him. "I missed you too."

The words were entirely insufficient to express what I really felt. I lifted a finger to trace his brows again, dragging it down the other side of his face. When my thumb traced his lip, he caught it in his teeth, sucking it lightly. Need barreled through me, my channel clenching, and my body aflame. I didn't know what to do other than tumble into the fire. I started to lean toward him again, but his hand dropped from my cheek, gently gripping my shoulder and holding me in place.

"I don't want to rush," he said.

It wasn't that I wanted to rush, it was more that I was so overcome with the moment I could hardly contain myself.

Yet, in the midst of the maelstrom when I could've been an utter disaster inside, I wasn't. Because with Caleb, I felt safe for the first time in years.

I managed a shuddering breath and nodded. As I stood between the cage of his knees, his hands slid down my arms, reaching to unbutton my blouse. With the flames of the fire flickering behind us, he slowly began to undress me. It was only when my blouse started to fall off of my shoulders that I recalled he had never seen my scars. In a panic, I caught the edges of my blouse, tugging it closed again.

My panic must've shown on my face. His eyes flicked to mine, his hands stilling where they rested at the buttons of my jeans. "What?" he asked, his voice intent and gentle.

Words lodged in my throat, so I did the only thing I could and slowly released my blouse and let it fall open, exposing the scars on my side and abdomen.

Maybe it didn't make sense, but the scars were the easiest part of everything that had happened. Don't mistake that for me saying that healing from burns was easy. Hell no. It was more like walking through fire again and again and again. The worst of the scars were on my left side where I'd sustained burns on the side of my waist that wrapped around to the front and back. The scarred area spanned from just below my breast to the edge of my pelvic bone. There was a gap of unblemished skin and then another swath of scarring on the side of my upper thigh. I also had scarring in small areas on my back and arms. Those were small enough to not be so obvious. When burns healed, the skin looked stretched tight and almost shiny.

Caleb's eyes hadn't left my face yet. My mind spun back to those first few years after the accident when I was a little wild and reckless, busy trying to forget everything. One night stands were my thing. Not that I had that many of them, mind you. But here and there, when the grief got too much, when the guilt of surviving sliced through me and when I just wanted to forget, I would try to escape with enough alcohol to blunt everything I felt and find someone to hold me.

I wasn't ashamed of my scars, but I had become sadly

accustomed to the reaction of others when they saw them. It wasn't pretty, and it could've been so much worse. I'd never forget this man who was in the burn unit in Anchorage at the same time I was. Like me, he'd been in a car accident, but it had been much worse and he had no Caleb there to pull him out to safety. He'd sustained burns over much of his body. In the face of that, he was the most cheerful person I'd ever met. Even in severe pain, his spirit had shone through. His wife had said hello to me one day when she was there visiting, and we struck up a conversation. His life changed drastically because of the accident. Yet, they were still married, and we'd stayed in touch over the years.

Meeting him at that time had helped me immensely. While I had struggled with all of my feelings about Jake dying and the mess of it all, I'd actually done okay when it came to accepting my scars. Beauty was only skin deep, and I knew that. Despite that, I carried a sense of trepidation whenever someone was going to see my body.

"I just didn't want you to be startled," I finally said in response to his question.

I wouldn't pretend I wasn't self-conscious at all, because I was, but it was from my worry over how he might react. His eyes flicked down finally as I let go of my blouse and it slid to the floor. I watched him carefully, trying to read into what might be passing through his mind.

He lifted a hand, tracing along the top edge of where the scarring began along my ribs. His hand came to rest in the dip at my waist after he traced all the way down to where the scars disappeared below the waistband of my jeans. Only then did he look back to me again. His eyes gleamed with a hint of tears, but there was no disgust, no shock, simply acceptance.

"I wish you'd let me be there for you," he said, his voice breaking into the weighted quiet.

"I wasn't ready. If I could do it all over, I would."

I meant those words with every fiber of my heart. I could

only wonder if everything would've been different if I hadn't nearly lost my mind with grief and shock and pushed away everyone who mattered for those first few years. Maybe I wouldn't have ended up in Oregon, maybe I wouldn't have had a crazy idiot become obsessed with me. Yet, there was one thing I had learned in therapy—I had to accept what happened. So I was trying. I couldn't change my past, but I might be able to change my future.

Caleb never looked away and nodded slowly. "Can you feel this?" he asked.

I felt the brush of his thumb against my skin over the scars. The sensation wasn't the same as if he'd been brushing over my unscarred skin, but I could still feel it. A true gift.

At my nod, his hand slid down over my scars, coming to rest just above the curve my hip. As we stared at each other, the air around us hummed, and the butterflies unleashed in my belly went wild.

"I'm sorry I wasn't there," he murmured.

Emotion and desire were barreling through me, twisting and tangling together.

I shook my head. "I pushed you away. It wasn't your fault."

Something flickered in the depths of his eyes. In this moment, so fraught with emotion, need, uncertainty, and the ghosts of our shared past, I couldn't have interpreted it if I tried.

"But I could've argued about it. I could've pushed back."

"It doesn't matter now. Just like we can't change what happened that night, we can't change what happened after."

Lifting his hand, he brushed my hair away from my forehead, lightly tracing the stitches along my hairline. "When do you see the doctor again?"

"Tomorrow actually."

Tucking a loose lock of hair behind my ear, he threaded his hand into my hair. Then, his lips were on mine again, and I forgot everything else.

His tongue tangled with mine, while my hands got busy. I needed more, I needed everything, everywhere, all at once. I wanted to tumble into this madness, every searing minute of it. When I moaned into our kiss, he broke free, his lips blazing a wet trail down the side of my neck.

"Off," I demanded, yanking at his shirt. I needed to feel his skin against mine. With a low chuckle, he lifted his head. Reaching behind his neck, he lifted his T-shirt off in one swoop where it fell to the floor with my blouse.

His palm slid down the center of my spine in a heated pass. Cupping my bottom, he pulled me tight against him. The feel of his body against mine elicited a gasp from me. My skin felt alive, little fires lighting under the surface at every point of contact.

His lips made their way down into the valley between my breasts, creating a pocket of space between us. He cupped a breast, his thumb teasing my nipple, while he dragged his tongue over the other. His teeth scored me lightly, my nipples puckering to an ache.

I cried out when he lifted his head. "Don't stop," I gasped.

But then he was lifting me against him. I curled my legs around his hips as he turned. He held me easily, his strength evident. Walking swiftly across the room, he carried me up the spiral staircase without once missing a step. With his hard cock at the apex of my thighs, rubbing against my core, the friction of the denim between us made me wild. I drew my tongue along the side of his neck, savoring the salty tang of his skin. Breathing in deeply, I inhaled his scent, so familiar it was like a drug.

Before I knew it, we were upstairs in his bedroom and he was easing me down onto his bed.

"Ella."

My eyes flickered open to find him, the heat of his gaze like a brand. He took my breath away. My eyes coasted over his body—every inch of it so muscled, he might as well have been carved from stone. I lingered on a few scars on his forearms, recognizing them as the burn scars from our accident.

Leaning up on my elbows, I reached for the button on his jeans. He moved quickly, taking a step back and kicking off his boots. In no time, he stood in front of me in nothing but a pair of fitted black briefs, his arousal evident. My channel clenched, and I became acutely aware of the drenched silk between my thighs.

He nudged my thighs apart with his knee, his fingers trailing under the curve of my breasts. As gentle as his touch was, it sent slivers of fire through me.

"Caleb," I murmured.

"Ella," was his only reply.

I had no idea what I might've meant to say. Losing all sense of anything other than the feel of him near me and the intimacy catching us in its web, I sank into a haze of need. His touch dusted over my belly before he swiftly unbuttoned my jeans and slid them off my hips. On the heels of the gentle sound of the fabric tumbling to the floor, he stretched out over me. His lips met mine in another searing kiss. His lips were everywhere—on my neck, down over my breasts, teasing my nipples.

He dusted soft kisses over the curve of my belly and then on my side. In the years since the accident, no one had ever touched my scars other than me, or nurses and doctors. Caleb did. He traced along the edges, the contrast of the subtly ticklish sensation over the scars and the feel of his lips on the unmarred surface of my skin shattering me with need.

"Ella."

I dragged my eyes open at the gruff sound of my name. Lifting my head, I met his gaze, the look there so intent, so strong, it arrowed into my heart, straight to the core I'd buried behind walls and numbness. Tears pricked at my eyes again. For a moment, sheer terror struck me, and I almost pushed back. But I couldn't.

This was Caleb. This was me. Us.

With Caleb's eyes locked to mine, he dragged his fingers across the damp silk between my thighs.

That was what I needed, pure sensation to make me forget, to push me through to the other side of everything I'd hidden from. My hips reflexively arched into his touch, my head falling back. Rolling to my side, he dragged my panties down, and I kicked them free from my ankles.

Then, his fingers were stroking through my slick folds. I gasped at each pass, my sex clenching. I heard myself murmuring his name again and again—that seemed to be the only word I was capable of speaking now.

Caleb's mouth came against me as a finger sank into my channel. He had always been a generous lover. Our teenage explorations had been awkward at times, but always fun. I knew he would tease and dally without ever getting impatient, but I was too close to the edge to make that possible. My hips flexed into him as a second finger joined the first, both of them buried deep inside of me while his tongue teased over my clit.

Pressure gathered inside, swirling in my core, narrowing to a point of sensation at my center. Pleasure scored through me, hard and fast, with every swirl of his tongue and every drive of his fingers inside of me. I broke apart, pleasure piercing me from the inside out.

I felt him slowly pull back and stand. Dragging my eyes open, I glanced up to see him kicking his briefs off, all of him now bared to me. I swallowed, need slamming into me again.

Every inch of him was pure muscle. He started to lean over me and then rolled to the side, reaching for his dresser. Inside of a hot second, he had a condom on and his weight was sinking down over me. The feel of him against me was so good, I almost cried out.

As he settled between my thighs, my legs curled around his hips and I rocked into him. The feel of his cock sliding through my folds almost sent me over the edge again.

"Ella," he murmured.

Opening my eyes, I found his gaze waiting, the look contained within them striking me at the heart. I'd forgotten many things, but I had never forgotten what it felt like to be this close to him. I felt vulnerable and safe at once. I swallowed against the emotion rising inside, trying to hold it together. Because I didn't want this to be a moment where he had to comfort me when I fell apart. Not when the only reason I was falling apart was because it felt so good to be with him again.

He brushed my tangled hair away from my face, saying more with his eyes than words could ever express. The need to cry subsided.

"I need to see you," he said simply.

I couldn't have denied him if I wanted to. And I didn't. Because I needed to see him too, to be present in this moment in a way I hadn't been in years.

He reached between us, adjusted the angle of his hips and surged into me. At the feel of him filling me, I gasped. Because I was tight. It had been a while.

Caleb held still for a beat, his hands curling into mine and gripping them tightly. With my breath heaving and his in tune with it, we stared at each other.

"I missed you," he repeated.

Chapter Ten

CALEB

Looking into Ella's eyes, I felt as if I had come home. But actually I'd never left. There had only ever been one woman with whom I felt like this. *Ella.* With her channel throbbing around me, enveloping me in her warm, creamy clench, and her skin damp against mine with her nipples tight little points against my chest, time felt as if it was collapsing into itself. The past fell away, the ten years we'd been apart were wiped out in a single moment.

My body took over because my need was that great. I drew back and sank into her again. With her legs curling around my hips as she arched up into me, I began a slow cycle of drawing back and sinking in. I managed to keep it under control at first, but that didn't last. Before I knew it I was pounding into her, savoring every cry, every gasp from her.

The need was quickening inside of me, tightening at the base of my spine, lashing at me. But I wasn't going to let go until she did again. I freed one of her hands and reached between us. One swirl of my thumb over her clit, and her channel pulsed around me. She cried out again, my name a chant.

I finally let go, my release crashing over me with such force I lost sight of everything but the feel of her channel milking my cock. I fell against her, rolling quickly so she was on top of me. Still buried deep inside of her, I slid my hand down her spine, my palm coming to rest on her bottom.

We lay still, my breath coming in heaves and emotion rocking me so hard, I almost cried. I tried to recall the last time I'd felt this intensely. The only memory that came to mind was when I saw her in the hospital ten years ago.

So many years wasted, but there was nothing to do other than be relieved she was here now. My hand had a mind of its own and started exploring her body again, sliding up her spine and easing down the soft curve of her side, savoring the swell of her breast into my palm. I reached the area where she carried scars.

She hadn't seemed self conscious about the scarring, but more worried about my reaction. I hated that. I couldn't help but wonder if someone had hurt her, reacted to the sight of her scars in a way that left a different kind of scar in its wake.

I traced along the edges of the area again and felt her lift her head. A smile curled her lips, eliciting one from me instantly.

Ella was quiet for a moment, her mossy green gaze searching mine. My heart thudded against my ribs, a visceral reminder of just how much she meant to me.

"Well," she said softly, her fingertips tracing along my collarbone.

"Well what?"

Her cheeks flushed a deeper shade of pink, and she shrugged. "I don't know. That was just..." Her words trailed off.

"Amazing?"

She smiled, and my cock twitched, which was a damn miracle.

I slid up against the pillows and lifted her against me, standing and striding into the bathroom. When I'd impulsively texted her earlier, I'd had no clue if she'd agree to meet me for dinner. When she had, I'd raced over to meet her without having a chance to shower after work.

"Where are we going?" she asked, a giggle escaping.

"Shower," I replied as I walked through the archway into the bathroom.

I'd never have considered myself one for luxury, but I loved this bathroom. When Owen and Ivy showed me the house design, I had initially scoffed at the bathroom plans, thinking they were too much. But Owen had assured me I'd love it, and I did. I reluctantly eased Ella down just outside the shower.

Disposing of my condom, I reached inside to turn the water on. Inside of a few seconds, steam was filling the bathroom, and I tugged Ella into the shower with me. She glanced up at the two showerheads directly in the ceiling sending a rainfall of water over us.

"Oh my. This is nice," she murmured.

Reaching around her, I turned on a few more jets along the tiled walls. She looked over with a laugh. "I bet you love this after work."

"Absolutely. Owen had to talk me into it because I thought it was a little ridiculous at first. Now I wouldn't trade it for the world."

I couldn't help but watch as she soaped up. I'd have thought myself long past the age where my control was an issue, but with Ella standing there with water and bubbles sluicing over her skin, it was fair to say control wasn't my strength. I felt my cock swelling and had to turn away, snagging the shampoo and focusing on anything but her.

When I had control of my body again, I turned around to see her leaning back, rinsing her hair. I let myself just soak in the sight of her. Her dark brown hair cascaded down her back. She had a lithe, strong build. There was more lushness to her now with her hips and her breasts fuller. I hadn't even noticed the scarring on her thigh earlier. A vivid memory flashed through my thoughts.

The dark, cold night I'd pulled her from the car, she'd been on her side. I remembered it so clearly, yet it wasn't something I allowed myself to dwell on. While the accident itself was horrible, it was everything that happened afterwards that was so painful—the shock of Jake's death and the fear that Ella might not make it through. They'd stabilized her the first night at the hospital, but the doctors kept warning of the possibility of infection.

Now, so many years later, only the scarring on her side and thigh would let anyone know something like that had happened. Moving on instinct, I stepped to her, sliding my hands down her sides onto her hips.

With a sputter, she opened her eyes, her lashes spiky from the water. Just like that, the space around us hummed. I wouldn't deny my desire, but desire wasn't what this moment was about.

"You're so beautiful," I murmured.

Her eyes widened and her lips parted. After a beat, she spoke. "You don't mind?"

"Mind what?"

She slid her hands down, resting one just above the scarring on her side. "This."

"Ella, I don't give a damn. If you're worried about how it looks, you're just beautiful as you ever were. This just tells the story of everything you've been through."

She stared at me, as if trying to read into something that wasn't there.

"Do you mind?" I finally asked, confused if only because she didn't seem self-conscious about it.

She shook her head. "No, but..." She paused, biting the

corner of her lip. "Well, some people do and I don't want it to be...."

Anger flashed through me. I wouldn't have expected her to not be with anyone when we were apart. Hell, I might've missed her so much it was an ache in my heart I'd simply learned to live with, but I had my fair share of dates and attempted relationships. Yet, her reaction only made me wonder again how others must've reacted to the sight of her scars.

To me, her scars made her more beautiful. They didn't matter one fucking bit.

She read my expression and shook her head again. "It's just that they make some people uncomfortable. Don't go getting angry with no one who's here and no one who matters. I just needed to know if it mattered for you."

"Never."

Chapter Eleven

CALEB

The heat of the sun angling across the bed woke me. For a hazy moment, I was confused. I felt the warm, lush body curled up against me and a leg tucked in between mine. As consciousness filtered in and my brain came online, I remembered

Ella was here.

With me.

It suddenly occurred to me that I'd never actually spent the night with her. You don't really get a chance to do that in high school, unless your parents aren't paying attention, or you're sneaky enough to pull it off somehow.

I couldn't say I never tried to persuade Ella on that account, but I'd never gotten away with it. Willow Brook was small, and her father was the police chief. She'd reminded me time and again, there were no secrets for her and she hadn't wanted to face her parents' disappointment.

I opened my eyes to find her head against my shoulder with her hair spread out over the pillow behind her. It was longer than I'd remembered. The last time I'd seen her before she moved back, she'd been wearing it in a bob. Now, it almost reached her waist—a rich cascade of mahogany, long enough for me to grip in my fists, just as I had last night when we crawled back in bed after our shower.

She was naked, and my cock was well aware of that fact. Her breasts pushed against my side, and I could feel the soft rise and fall of her breath where my palm rested against her back. I couldn't resist sliding it down over the dip in her low back and cupping the sweet curve of her ass. My naughty thoughts were interrupted by Creamsicle.

He was above sleeping in my bed and always had been, but he usually expected me up and about by now. He leapt onto the foot of the bed with a meow. When I glanced up, I found him sitting on his haunches, his tail twitching back and forth over the comforter.

Ella shifted, murmuring something against my shoulder. The feel of her lips moving against my skin in a way that had nothing to do with sex sent a shot of blood straight to my groin.

With Creamsicle's gaze upon us, I asked, "Yes?"

"What's that?" she asked, her voice coming out more clearly this time.

"That's Creamsicle," I replied with a chuckle.

Glancing to her, I found her eyes opening. Sweet hell. She was dangerous in the morning. With her hair tousled, her skin slightly flushed and her eyes sleepy, all I wanted was to spend all day in bed with her. In fact, I'd have been quite happy to make up for ten years of lost time right now.

She rose up on her elbow, the sheet sliding down as she did. My eyes went straight to her breasts. Her nipples were dusky pink, the lush curves calling to me. Before I even realized what I was doing, I had caught one of her nipples with my lips, giving it a quick suck.

She squealed and then giggled, and my heart clenched. "He's watching us!" she exclaimed, swatting me on the head.

Drawing back, I rested against the pillows and looked

over at Creamsicle. He was unimpressed and let out a meow. "I think he's out of food," I said, glancing to Ella as I slid my palm up her back to sift through her tousled hair.

"Well then you should feed him. Come on, I'll make breakfast."

Before I could argue against it, she was climbing out of bed. With my cock protesting, I gamely went along with her. At this point, I would do just about anything Ella wanted.

In short order, we were downstairs in the kitchen. She wore one of my T-shirts, which hung almost to her knees, and a pair of socks. Meanwhile, I'd tossed on a pair of sweat-pants and nothing else. While I filled Creamsicle's food bowl, Ella padded around the kitchen opening cabinets and checking everything out. I turned around, walking with Creamsicle's water bowl, to find her leaning up on her tiptoes trying to reach for some coffee mugs that were just out of her reach. Distracted by the T-shirt rising up and offering a tantalizing glimpse of the sweet curve of her bottom, my cock responded in kind. She had on a pair of purple silk panties. Fuck me.

She'd grumbled that she needed to get home and change. Amongst other things I hadn't planned on with our impromptu dinner last night was a change of clothes for her. If I had my way, she'd pack a bag tonight and just stay with me. Yet, as comfortable as last night had been, I sensed I needed to take things one step at a time. For my own sake, as well as hers.

"Hang on, let me get that," I said, setting the water bowl on the counter as I stepped past her. Without an ounce of hesitation, I stretched up behind her, sliding my hands over her hips and dropping a kiss in the curve of her neck. I savored her soft gasp. Only then did I reach up and get the coffee mugs down, thinking to myself I hadn't organized my kitchen with anyone other than myself in mind. I topped six feet, two inches, while Ella was almost a foot shorter.

Reluctantly stepping away from her, I handed her the

coffee mugs before filling Creamsicle's water bowl. Ella started coffee, and before I'd even returned to the kitchen, she had the refrigerator open and was looking inside. "Can I make omelets?" she called.

Creamsicle scurried past me and started wolfing down his food. "You can make whatever you want," I said as I reached the counter opposite her. She let the door to the refrigerator fall closed and turned around, resting her hips against the counter beside it.

"Well you have eggs, milk and some cheese. You have a terrible selection of vegetables though," she offered with a sly grin.

I knew perfectly well that I had no vegetables, at least not in the fridge. I shrugged, unabashed. "Look, I've never been much of a cook, but then you know that."

She grinned. "I do. Your mom used to complain that you hated learning to cook. If it's okay, then I'll make omelets."

At my nod, she got started. The next hour passed in a strange sense of comfort. I'd never had a morning like this with Ella. Yet, it felt as though I had. She made the coffee strong, just how I liked it. Though the omelets were simple, they were delicious.

It was only when my phone started ringing that I was snapped out of my reverie. Taking a swig of my coffee, I glanced over to her. "That's my phone. Do you want me to get it?" I asked, recalling I'd turned my phone over to her.

Clouds passed through her eyes, and I recalled what had prompted me to offer for us to switch phones temporarily. Inside of a matter of seconds, the relaxed expression on her face had fallen away, her gaze haunted.

Fuck. This needed to be resolved and fast. I didn't think I could take seeing Ella like that.

"Why don't you get it? It's not like anyone knows to call my number to reach you." She slipped off the stool across from me, padding across the floor. My gaze tracked her because it was impossible not to look at her. I loved that she was wearing my T-shirt.

By the time she returned with my phone, it stopped ringing. I slid it over and saw Nate's number on the screen. "I'll call him later. I'm gonna have to explain to everybody that you have my phone right now. Will that be okay?"

"It feels funny, but it's such a relief to know you'll have my phone. I'd rather deal with everybody thinking I'm crazy than deal with that," she said softly.

The anger I'd forgotten about last night in the heat of everything else came roaring back, hot and then icy cold. "Ella, when did all of this start?"

She lifted her mug off the counter and spun away to refill it. "Need some?"

When I shook my head, she turned back and slipped onto the stool across from me, finally answering. "About a year and a half ago. I accepted the job there two years ago, right at the start of the fall semester. After a few months, he asked me out. Not that I'd done anything to lead him on. I said no, thinking he'd drop it after that. That's when things started. It seems to come in waves. Like there would be nothing for a month or so, and then out of nowhere it would happen again. In a way, that makes it worse because I can never relax. Just when I start to think it will stop, it starts up."

Her eyes met mine, her gaze earnest as if though she needed to convince me of something. "I meant it last night. I really did want to come home anyway. I thought I'd found my dream job, but where you live is everything, right? I just kept thinking I would wait for the right time or find the right job here before I came home. Then, all this started up and it seemed like it was better if I just cut my losses. Funny thing was, once I made the decision, then the job here opened up."

I stared at her, trying to collect my thoughts. Because the only thing I could think when I thought about what this guy had done and was still doing was I wanted to make him fucking pay. But Ella didn't need to see my fury. I slid my phone across the counter to her. Cupping her coffee mug in her hands, she took a sip on the heels of a deep breath.

"It's so embarrassing, but now that you know and my mom knows, I'm relieved. I have friends there, and they wanted to help, but it wasn't the same. Portland's a pretty big city. Do you think he'll just drop it eventually now that I'm gone?" she asked, as if I could actually answer that for her.

I hated the look in her eyes—haunted and weary. I desperately wanted to give her the answer she wanted to hear, but I couldn't. "I don't know, Ella. I hope so. I hope your dad can give us some suggestions on how to hold him accountable." I couldn't bring myself to say the guy's name aloud, although it was seared into my memory—Lance Wallace.

Ella took another sip of coffee, idly tracing circles on the counter. Creamsicle leapt up, padding cross the counter and stopping beside her. He couldn't have known how perfect his timing was, or perhaps he did know. Nevertheless, he interrupted our conversation. Considering that I liked to solve things, and this issue wasn't one I could solve quickly, his interruption was welcome.

Ella glanced to him and then me, a slight smile crossing her face. "He's allowed on the counter?"

I chuckled. "I tried to train him off of it, but I'm not very good at training cats apparently. It probably doesn't help that in the summers I'm gone for weeks at a time and he has the run of the house. My mom stops by twice a day. One time, my mom brought him over to their place, but he hated it so she brought him back over here. He's got a cat door in the laundry room, so he runs the show when I'm not here. My vet told me he considers this his territory."

Ella stroked her palm down his back and rubbed his cheeks, eliciting a loud purr from him. Meanwhile, my heart clenched and I hated to have our idyllic morning interrupted by the memory of those nasty texts last night. As much as they rattled me, it was stunning to consider that Ella had been dealing with it for over a year and a half now. I'd be stopping by to chat with Rex soon as I could today.

Chapter Twelve

CALEB

Early that afternoon, I pushed through the swinging door between the fire station and the police station. Willow Brook Fire & Rescue was smack in the middle of downtown on Main Street. After my lazy morning with Ella, I'd headed into the station to respond to a local fire. In the off-season as a hotshot firefighter, we were still on duty for local fires and could still be called out to anywhere across Alaska if we were needed, but the summer season was the busiest time of year for us. My plan to talk to Rex right away had been put off while we dealt with the fire. No shock, but it was a wood-stove chimney fire. Every fall, people started using their woodstoves, many not bothering to clean the stove pipe chimney. Leftover build up from the winter before, or debris left from wild animals nesting in them easily caught fire.

After a quick shower once we were done, I went over to talk with Rex. Lightly knocking the back of my knuckles on the door, I called out, "Rex, you got a few?"

Rex Masters glanced up, a smile stretching across his face. "Come on in. Good to see you, Caleb," he said with a wave.

"Always good to see you, Rex," I replied. As he lifted up a coffee cup and then glanced into it with a frown, I asked, "Need a fresh cup of coffee?"

"That would be great," he replied with a wink.

I stepped out and into the small break room across from his office, finding a full pot of fresh coffee there. Maisie, the station's dispatcher, spoiled Rex rotten.

Returning with the two cups of coffee, I glanced over. "Mind if I close the door?"

Rex's eyes narrowed, but he shook his head. I gathered he might be wondering why we needed privacy. Handing over his coffee, I closed the door and sat down across from his desk.

"I'm guessing Ella was with you last night," he offered by way of greeting.

I almost choked on the sip of coffee I'd just taken. It wasn't that I would've hidden anything from Rex, or from anyone for that matter, but he *was* her father. While I knew perfectly well she was approaching twenty-seven years old, it didn't change the fact I didn't particularly want to chat with *her* father about Ella spending the night with me. Not to mention, my feelings for her were miles and miles and miles away from being platonic.

Rex chuckled and shrugged. "She's a grown woman, and I always liked you." Without waiting for me to reply, he continued, "Let me guess, you're here to talk to me about that asshole who's been stalking her online."

"Damn good guess. She mentioned she talked to her mom about it yesterday, so I figured Georgia talked to you."

Rex leaned back in his chair, taking a sip of his coffee, his gaze considering. "Georgia's fit to be tied about it, and I'm furious."

"I'm fucking furious too. I wish Ella had said something sooner."

Rex gestured toward his computer. "I just heard back from a guy I emailed down at the Portland Police Department this morning. I've asked him to send up Lance Wallace's records there and whatever police reports Ella made about him. I'll talk to Ella later today when I get home. I'm pissed they didn't do more to help her, but I'll see what I can do with what they have. He might not be in my jurisdiction now, but she is. I've also put a call in to my buddy in the Anchorage unit who deals with online crimes across state lines. How much did she tell you?"

I pulled her phone out of my pocket. Before we went our separate ways this morning, I had her check to see if there was anything on it she didn't want me to see. She'd laughed and said she led a rather boring life. Aside from texts with family and friends, that was it. Pulling up the texts that showed up last night from Lance, I spun the phone around on his desk and slid it across to him.

"These showed up while we were having dinner. She didn't want to tell me about it at first, but she did. We traded phones."

It didn't appear Rex heard a word I said. He was scrolling through the messages, his gaze darkening with anger as he read them. He glanced up. "What the hell? I cannot believe this has been going on for almost two years." He ran a hand through his hair with a ragged sigh. "She's been through too much already. No one deserves this kind of bullshit."

It went without question that I understood exactly how he was feeling. I could imagine, as her father, his concerns and worries for her had their own weight.

"Why do you have her phone?" he belatedly asked. As I'd guessed, he hadn't heard my comment.

"My idea. I suggested we trade phones. You guys know how to reach me, so that's how you reach her now. I figure this way she doesn't have to see his bullshit. I don't want her worrying about it. Any suggestions on how I should respond?"

Rex's dark expression dissolved when he burst out laughing. "Fucking brilliant. But then you always were a smart kid," he offered with an arch of his brow. Pausing, he took another sip of coffee. "Let me talk to my guy in Anchorage. I'd love to find a way to nail this guy with some charges. In the meantime, I'd say don't respond at all. I know you'll want to, but let's not stir the pot. Make sure to save the messages and don't respond to them. Actually, anytime he contacts that phone in any way, forward it to me."

When he slid the phone back across the desk, I quickly forwarded the messages to him. I hadn't discussed this with Ella—mostly because I didn't want her to worry more than she already had—but I knew it wouldn't be easy *not* to reply. I wanted to tell the guy to go to fucking hell. But, I'd do whatever Rex suggested for now.

Taking a gulp of my coffee, I set the cup down on the armrest of the chair, curling my hand around it as I looked over at him. "It won't be easy, but I'll do it. I don't want her to see any more of this shit from him, so any thoughts on how to deal with her emails?"

"Yeah Georgia mentioned those too. When I see her tonight, I'll ask if she'll forward the emails directly to me. He won't know they're being forwarded, but that way they can be on the record. Usually, assholes like this don't do anything in person. It's all about messing with people's heads. I'm hoping now that she's here, we can make this stop for once and for all. I'm not going to just sit back and wait though. This guy needs to be charged and I'll find a way to make it happen."

"I'm so glad she finally told us what the hell was going on," I replied, running a hand through my hair. Just talking about it sent a fresh wave of anger and frustration through me. I hated knowing this guy had been pulling this shit— leaving her scared and creeped out.

Rex nodded. "You keep me in the loop, I'll keep you in the loop. We'll figure this out. With her having your phone, everyone's gonna have to know what's going on," he said with a chuckle.

I shrugged. "I know. She pointed that out too, but she said she didn't care."

Rex eyed me for a beat, his gaze considering. "I'm glad you two reconnected," he finally said.

I didn't want things to get awkward. I'd have bet his idea of how we reconnected and mine were probably quite different. I was saved from wondering how to navigate this topic when the station intercom went off, reporting an accident on the highway on the outskirts of town.

Rex and I both shifted gears, parting ways to respond to the call. As I drove out with a small crew, I realized I was passing through the same section where I'd seen Ella's car turned over in the ditch. More than a week had passed since then. I couldn't have known she'd waltz back into my world and turn it upside down.

Chapter Thirteen

ELLA

"Ella?" a voice called.

Glancing up, a doctor I'd never met was standing by the door to the reception area at the doctor's office. When I met her eyes, she smiled, a hint of a question in her gaze.

I stood from my chair, setting aside the magazine I'd been flipping through. "That's me," I said, giving a little wave as I approached her.

After I'd left the hospital from my roll in the ditch, the hospital had automatically scheduled an appointment here for me. This was the one and only general medical clinic in Willow Brook. I hadn't been here in years. Willow Brook Family Medicine had expanded from one doctor to two, or so it appeared. I'd been expecting to see Dr. Johnson, although by my calculations he had to be approaching seventy at this point.

When I reached the woman, she held out her hand with another smile. "Hi Ella, I'm Dr. Charlie Lane. Please just call me Charlie."

"Nice to meet you. I'm Ella, but you already know that," I replied with a quick shake of her hand.

Gesturing me through the door, she closed it behind us. "Come on back. I understand you're here to get some stitches removed."

"That's the plan. They said it would be up to you to see if they were ready to be removed."

I followed her into a small room, and she closed the door, gesturing for me to sit in a chair beside a narrow counter against the wall. She slipped her hips onto a rolling stool with an attached table and computer monitor.

As she clicked through a few screens, I glanced over at her. She had to be the youngest doctor I'd ever met, or so I guessed. She had dark hair with a whimsical streak of purple on one side and wide gray eyes behind her glasses. She wore a white lab coat and gave off an air of seriousness.

"Looks like you've been a patient here since you were a little girl," she commented.

"Well, it's the only clinic in town. I think Dr. Johnson was everybody's doctor, right? Obviously, you're new. With you here and all the upgrades, this place is totally different," I observed.

The entire office had been updated with fresh paint and new furnishings. Charlie nodded and smiled softly.

"I am new here. I actually moved here from Boston. I always wanted to come to Alaska. When I saw this job, I jumped at it. I was actually born in Alaska when my dad was stationed here in the military. My parents moved away before I even started kindergarten, but it's always been my dream to come back."

"Are you planning to stay?" I asked.

She nodded, her gray eyes brightening. "I love it here. Willow Brook is ideal. It's small, and it feels like we're in the middle of nowhere, but we're not too far away from Anchorage, so I can get my city fix if I need it."

"Exactly why I love it here too. Have you survived a winter yet though?"

Charlie shook her head and smiled. "Not yet. Boston

definitely has winter, but I understand it'll be longer and darker here. I'm optimistic I can handle it just fine. Anyway, let me take a look at those stitches. Before we get to that, I have to do the usual and clear a few standard questions."

At my nod, she quickly asked me a run of questions, checked my blood pressure, weighed me and asked me if anything had changed since the last time I had seen a doctor. She didn't say a word about my car accident ten years ago. It was a bit of a relief. For a while there, every time I went to the doctor that came up. But it had been long enough now that there wasn't anything else left to ask.

After that process, she gestured for me to sit on the examining table. Stepping to my side, she carefully brushed my hair back from my forehead to check the stitches. "Looks good. You ready for me to do this?"

"Let's do it."

She quickly removed them, so fast I barely felt a thing.

"No bleeding," she commented as she carefully dabbed the area with antiseptic. "No need for a bandage unless you want one. I'd recommend you use this cream over the scar for a few days," she said as she handed me a tube of cream. "Be careful when you're washing your face and things like that. The skin will still be tender for a few more days, but it's healed up nicely. You shouldn't even notice the scar once it completely heals."

"That's what I was hoping," I said. "Anything else?"

She shook her head. "Nope. You're done for the day."

"Well, it was nice to meet you," I said as she walked me back down the hall. "I suppose I'll be seeing you for anything standard from this point going forward."

With a smile, she nodded, stepping out into the waiting room with me. Once I turned away from her, my gaze landed on Jesse Franklin. Jesse was a friend of Cade's, and I'd known him for years. While he hadn't grown up here, his family moved here while I was still in high school after Cade had graduated. They'd become fast friends and stayed in touch even when Cade moved away for a while. "Jesse!" I exclaimed as soon as I saw him. "What are you doing here?"

Along with being a friend of Cade's, Jesse was also a hotshot firefighter. He flashed a roguish grin. "Just stopping to get my shoulder checked out. I dislocated it last week out in the field," he explained, rolling his shoulder as he spoke.

He gave me a quick hug when I reached him, ruffling my hair as I stepped away. He was as handsome as ever with his dark amber hair and green eyes that usually held a twinkle. He was like a brother to me. "Good to see you," I murmured.

"Good to have you back. Your dad and Cade are tickled," he replied with a wink.

Turning to say goodbye to Charlie, I noticed she'd gone quiet and her cheeks were flushed. Meanwhile, Jesse's usual teasing demeanor faded when he glanced her way. "Dr. Lane," he said with a nod. "I'm not late this time."

Dr. Lane, or rather Charlie as she'd asked me to call her, didn't seem as relaxed with Jesse as she had with me. In fact, she seemed downright tense.

"I'm hoping you're going to clear me to go back to duty today," Jesse added.

Uncertain how to read what was going on, I figured it was best for me to go. I waved goodbye to both of them and slipped out.

Chapter Fourteen

ELLA

A short drive later, I walked into Firehouse Café. I'd made plans to meet Holly for coffee this afternoon. Stepping inside, I didn't even get a chance to look around before Janet was calling my name. She was walking by with a tray of dishes and looped her hand through my elbow.

"Hello Ella!" She squeezed my arm with her greeting and next thing I knew I was in the kitchen with her as she emptied the dishes into a tray in the dishwasher area.

"Who are you meeting for coffee today?" she asked.

I grinned. Her enthusiasm was infectious. "Holly. I didn't even get a chance to see if she was here yet."

Janet brushed a loose lock of her salt and pepper hair out of her eyes and shook her head. "Nope, she's not here yet. I can go ahead and get your coffee though."

"Don't you need to be out front?" I asked with a low chuckle.

"Oh right," she said with a laugh, immediately pushing past me through the swinging doors to the front. A young man was busy at the dishwasher and a young woman was busy at the grill. Janet always managed the counter here, one of the reasons I loved coming here. She had a way of brightening my day.

Janet was a good friend of my parents, but then I supposed she was a good friend of everyone in town. Firehouse Café was a mainstay in Willow Brook, in part because of Janet. She was nosy and tended toward bossy, but she was warm and kind-hearted and would do just about anything for a friend in need.

Following her back out into the café, I rounded the counter as she immediately started talking to whoever happened to be waiting. Holly was stepping through the door as I walked to the back of the short line.

"Hey!" she said, pulling me in for a quick hug. "I'm going to hug you every time I see you for at least a year probably."

"I don't mind, not one bit," I replied with a laugh.

We turned to wait in line together. "So your stitches are out," she observed, her eyes flicking up to my hairline.

I hadn't even bothered to check to see how I looked before I left the doctor's office. I ran my fingers along the edge of my hairline, feeling the smooth surface of the fresh scar. "Yep, all gone. Dr. Lane seems nice. She asked me to call her Charlie. Have you met her yet?"

Holly nodded. "Yeah. I haven't had an appointment with her, but my mom did. I was there with her, and you know her, it was practically a job interview for the poor woman. Dr. Johnson is due to retire though, so I'm glad he found someone else. All the men in town are complaining though. I told Nate he should shut the hell up because Charlie's totally hot. I mean, they can either have an old geezer checking them out, or a hot chick who's smart as hell. Take your pick."

I burst out laughing. "She's pretty hot, but I doubt the guys want to think about that when she's checking on their rash or whatever."

Holly rolled her eyes. "I know. Men are just not used to the doctor thing. They avoid it like the plague."

We made it to the front of the line, and Janet smiled widely. As if though she hadn't just seen me minutes ago. "Hi girls, what can I get for you?"

"I'll take a shot in the dark," I replied.

Holly rolled her eyes. "You and your badass coffee. I'll take a mocha with toffee syrup and whipped cream."

"And you're aiming for a sugar coma?" I countered, enjoying how easily we'd fallen back into our old banter.

After we had our drinks, we snagged a table in the back corner. The tourist crowds were thinning out now that autumn was here, bringing cool days and frosty nights. Willow Brook, like many towns in Alaska, stayed very busy during the spring and summer. In particular, Willow Brook's proximity to Anchorage brought gobs of overflow tourists who enjoyed the convenience of Anchorage, but wanted a taste of the wilderness.

Yet, once the winds of autumn blew in, things tended to quiet down. Taking a deep breath, I glanced around the café, absorbing the feeling of just being home again. It wasn't as if I hadn't visited. Yet, it felt different knowing I was here to stay. I could appreciate being here in a way I hadn't during brief visits.

Holly started to say something when her phone buzzed. Holding her finger up for me to wait, she answered the call. I took a sip of my coffee and let my thoughts roll through the past twenty-four hours. I hadn't seen Holly since the other night at Wildlands when Caleb gave me a ride home. I was debating whether I wanted to share anything about Caleb with her just yet.

But Holly was my closest friend here, and I wasn't sure if I'd lost my mind by giving into my need for him last night. In fact, I felt half crazy. Everything was so much more intense than it had ever felt before. So many of my memories from our youthful love had been swamped by the accident. Now, I felt like a foolish schoolgirl. So foolish that if

Caleb had asked me to marry him this morning, I probably would've said yes.

Yet, I didn't know if I was thinking clearly, and I couldn't shake the feeling I didn't deserve to have Caleb. It wasn't just how good it felt to be with him – so amazing I couldn't even put words to it — but that I felt so secure with him. The nagging fear that Lance had thrown into my life dissipated when I was with Caleb. I was convinced Caleb could hold my fear at bay. All of the self-doubt that had taken root so strongly in the last year or so made me question everything. Because, you see, I kind of had a thing about needing to take care of myself. Twined into that was the guilt that clung to me from the accident—guilt that I didn't deserve something good because Jake had died and somehow I should've been able to keep it from happening.

Logic wasn't winning this internal battle.

Once I'd finally been open about how deep my survivor's guilt ran, my therapist had gently pointed out that perhaps I should stop running from what I'd had with Caleb, that perhaps I was punishing myself when I broke up with him. I'd wanted to scream when she said that—if only because it was like she'd shined a light into the darkness I carried in my heart.

She'd pointed out the obvious fact we hadn't had closure. *Fuck closure* was about all I'd been able to muster about that. Everything had gotten so tangled up—there was the accident, survivor's guilt, my own serious injuries and the fact I'd had to rely heavily on my parents for a while, more so than I would have if I hadn't been injured. *Hovering* was insufficient to capture what it had been like the last two years of high school before I left for college.

There was all of that and then my academics, which had become a life raft for me. Lance with his creepy stalky behavior had managed to ruin the one thing that had been my oasis for so long. The one area of my life where I felt confident and in control was in my research and teaching.

He had muddied those waters so completely that even that didn't feel good anymore for me.

I gave myself a shake when Holly said my name. I'd been staring blankly out the window.

"I'm sorry, what was that?" I asked.

"Zoning out much?"

At my shrug, she continued. "Okay, let's get the crappy stuff out of the way first," Holly said, taking a big sip of her ridiculously sugary drink and leaning her elbows on the table.

"I have no idea how you drink that," I said, eyeing the whip cream drizzled with caramel and piled on top of her coffee.

Holly rolled her eyes. "Just like I have no idea how you deal with that bitter shit you like. Anyway, crappy stuff first."

Holly couldn't have known, but this almost made me cry. Not in the mood to burst into tears in the middle of town, I took a gulp of my coffee and the moment passed. *Crappy stuff first* was a rule we had made up back when we were much younger. The deal was if we had something hard to talk about, we had to do it first.

"Okay, what's the crappy stuff?"

"I can't believe you have to even ask that! The whole thing with your stalker guy. Please tell me you talked to your dad about it and please tell me he's on it."

This was definitely a crappy topic, but Caleb's idea for us to switch phones had made my life incredibly easier. It was such a small thing, but knowing I didn't have to worry about suddenly seeing a flurry of nasty texts was a massive relief. I figured now was as good a time as any to explain she'd need to call me on Caleb's number. Conveniently, she knew my parents' home phone number by heart, so she had called the house earlier today when I stopped by to change after my night with Caleb. I'd been beyond relieved both of my parents had already left for work.

"My mom talked to my dad. I was planning to talk to him more tonight."

Holly leaned back in her chair. "Have you heard from asshole again?"

"That's the thing. I don't know. I had dinner with Caleb last night, and I got a bunch of texts from Lance. Caleb saw them, and aside from the fact that he kind of freaked out, he suggested we switch phones. Maybe it's crazy, but now I won't even know. At first I thought it was a weird idea, but now I'm so relieved."

Holly's mouth fell open and then she gave her head a shake. "Caleb is fucking brilliant. But then I knew that, plus he adores you. All right, we don't have to dwell on it, but as long as you promise me you're going to talk to your dad, I'm good. And I'm going to call Caleb and thank him. I guess I can just call your number?"

"Yup. He's got it. It's my personal number, so I can just tell everybody here to call me on Caleb's and it'll be fine."

"Okay, crappy stuff over. You had dinner with Caleb last night?" Holly asked, moving on briskly.

I felt my cheeks heat, but I nodded. There was no sense in hiding this from Holly. This town was too small to try to hide much. I might not know what the best move was right now, but Holly was my friend and she would be honest with me.

"He texted me when I was on the way back from my day in Anchorage. So we had dinner," I explained.

Holly circled her hand in the air, taking another sip of her coffee and quickly wiping the whipped cream off of her upper lip with a napkin. "There's more to it than that because you're blushing," she said pointedly. "Please tell me this is some kind of amazing second chance thing. Pretty please. My love life sucks donkey, so I want to live vicariously through you."

"What do you mean? Are you..."

I meant to ask if she was okay, but Holly waved me off.

"Oh God. I'm fine. Just going through a looong dry spell, that's all. Back to you and Caleb. What happened?"

"I don't know what it is yet but, well, we spent the night together last night."

Holly squealed, and a few people looked our way.

"Would you keep it down? Please," I hissed.

Holly shrugged. "No one knows what we're talking about. Anyway, was it amazing?"

I felt my cheeks getting hot. Again. Having not spent too much time with Holly lately, I'd forgotten how direct she could be. Catching her sly gaze, I shook my head. "I'm not about to give you all the details here."

"Oh, I don't want all the details," she said with another wave of her hand. "Good god, that's weird. I just want to know if it was amazing."

I opened my mouth to say something and instead burst out laughing.

"I take it from how red your face is that it was," she offered with a wink. "Good. I always hated that you two broke up."

Despite the tragedy of Jake's death, Holly had faced it head on. That was a lesson I wish I had learned sooner. Now given the chance to do it over again, I wouldn't have tried to bury myself in ways to distract me from my grief. But I couldn't do it over. Back to my point though, Holly and I hadn't spoken much about my break up with Caleb in the aftermath of the accident.

At the time, she'd been dealing with her own grief just like all of us. Jake had been her boyfriend. It was hard to say how serious they'd been. With Jake his best friend and Holly mine, they were tossed into impromptu double dates all the time. A few months prior to the accident, they'd made their relationship more than just casual. Suffice it to say though, I hadn't felt right pouring my woes out to her about Caleb when she was muddling through her own grief.

The whole thing had been a tangled mess. Holding

myself to my new commitment to face things, I took a deep breath and met her gaze straight on. "What do you mean?"

"Look," she said, the sly grin fading from her face and her gaze sobering. "Back when everything happened, you were in the hospital, Jake was dead, and we were all hit hard by what happened. I'm not sure exactly what you were thinking, but I hated that you and Caleb broke up afterwards. We never really talked about it, and I understand why. I mean, I'm guessing you and pretty much the whole world were afraid to talk to me about anything else that might be hard."

I took a fortifying sip of coffee and nodded. "That about sums it up," I said softly.

Holly reached over and squeezed my hand. "I was a mess too. And I was scared for you. I mean, you were in the hospital for three weeks. That felt like forever back then. Once everything wasn't so crazy, I just felt sad that you and Caleb weren't together. You never told me why you guys broke up."

Even though therapy had helped me with a lot, I hadn't even considered how much had been left unsaid after the accident. I gave Holly's hand a squeeze and let it go. "I told him I thought we should take a break, and then we had a fight about it. Afterwards, it was like we kind of broke up with each other, although I started it. I was just... well, a mess and not thinking too clearly about anything. You're right too. We didn't talk about it after that. He graduated and left, and I just wanted to get through things."

Holly eyed me for a long moment, a rueful smile crossing her face. "I broke the rule," she said as she swirled some whip cream onto the end of her straw.

"What do you mean?"

"The crappy things first rule."

I shook my head. "This is a different kind of crappy. This is more just sad. None of us can bring Jake back, but I suppose we can maybe clear the air."

"No air needs to be cleared with me," Holly said emphatically. "I just wish you'd let go of it."

"Let go of what?" I asked obtusely, though I knew where she was going with this.

Holly stared at me for long enough that I shifted in my seat. Setting her coffee down, she leaned her elbows on the table. "Okay, here goes. We've talked about this before, but I'm done being nice about it. Every single time the accident comes up or I even mention Jake's name, you get this awful look on your face. I know you. I know you feel guilty, but you couldn't have stopped the accident. You know that! That guy crossed into our lane. No one could have changed what happened. No one."

Her eyes glistened with tears, and her words came out forcefully.

"Holly, I didn't mean..."

"You didn't upset me. Jake died. We all lost him. I just hate how you still feel bad. It's enough to grieve, but stop beating yourself up. Just stop it."

Staring at her, my thoughts circled. In my mind, I knew she was right. It was my heart I hadn't been able to convince. The tightness there eased just a little at the force of her words. Strangely, the weight I'd carried for so long felt a little lighter. Her frustration and clear hurt on my behalf somehow pierced through the guilt in a way that talking hadn't before.

On the heels of a deep breath and a fortifying sip of coffee, I managed to breathe through the emotion thick in my chest. "I'm trying. I really am. That's a big part of why I finally came home. If running wasn't going to fix it, I might as well try the opposite."

Holly was quiet, the fierce look in her eyes softening. "Good. I missed you like crazy."

We were quiet for a few moments. I savored my coffee and felt the intense emotion settle inside. She paused to take a few sips of her coffee concoction. After a moment, she caught my eyes, smiling softly. "Okay, back to Caleb. I'm glad you're giving him a chance again. I always thought you two were meant to be together." When my eyes widened, she nodded firmly. "Maybe it's silly, but it's true. Even with Jake, he was more of a friend than what you and Caleb were to each other. When I think back to high school, you two were about the only couple who really seemed like... I dunno, like it mattered."

My heart thudded suddenly. I wanted her to be right. My curiosity spiked. "So, has he been serious with anyone since I've been gone?"

Holly cocked her head to the side, drumming her fingertips on the table. "Well, he hasn't been here the whole time. I mean, he was gone for college, then he went away for training and was in Fairbanks for a while. I can't speak to any of that time, but I've never once heard he was serious with anyone. I wouldn't call him a player though. He dates here and there, but that's about it. He's hot as hell and there are plenty of women who would be happy to tie him up, but that's about it."

I couldn't help it, but a little thrill of satisfaction shot through me. It wasn't as if I thought I had a claim on him, but he'd always been tucked in the back of my thoughts—I'd wondered how he was doing and who would be lucky enough to catch him. It seemed no one yet.

On the heels of that, my thoughts sobered. Despite Holly's giddiness at the thought of Caleb and I getting back together, I couldn't think clearly about it. At all. My plan in coming home had been to simply try to come to some sort of peace. I'd had this idea we'd talk and take things slow. So much for that. I'd blown that up within a short week. I'd come skidding into town in a ditch—literally—and then stumbled right into Caleb's arms and the best sex I'd ever had in my life.

To say I was rushing into things might be an understatement. I looked over at Holly and sighed. "I might need to pump the brakes though."

"Why the hell do you need to do that?"

"Because it's been ten years, I just moved home, and I've got more than enough on my plate, including an asshole obsessed with me. I don't want to rush into anything."

"Sounds like the perfect time to lose yourself in some hot sex," Holly said bluntly.

I felt the heat rolling up my neck and face again. I took a gulp of coffee, throwing a glare at her.

She shrugged and rolled her eyes. "Oh, get over yourself. You don't have to solve world peace, you don't have to decide what's going to happen in the future right here and now. Maybe you could try to stop freaking out about everything."

At that moment, the bell above the door jingled, and I reflexively glanced over my shoulder. My older brother Cade and his wife Amelia walked through the door. They'd stopped by my parents' house a few times since I'd been home this week. I waved at Cade, and he caught my eye and winked, nudging his chin up. Amelia called over, "We'll be there in just a few."

Holly snagged an empty chair from a table nearby. Within a few minutes, Cade slipped into the chair beside me and Amelia beside Holly. Amelia beamed at me. "It is *so* awesome to have you home."

Cade and Amelia had gotten back together a few years ago after a messy break up years earlier. I'd been so relieved they'd found their way back to each other. Cade had been on the cranky side the entire time they'd been apart—which had been seven years by the way. Now they were back together, Amelia had softened him again.

I looked to him, nudging him with my elbow. "Hey Cade."

He glanced down, running a hand through his shaggy

brown curls, his green eyes crinkling at the corners with his grin. "Hey Ella."

Fleetingly, I wondered if our dad had filled Cade in on things with me. I hadn't seen my mother since our conversation yesterday, but I knew she talked to my dad because she'd texted me, and Caleb had forwarded the text to his phone. Shaking those thoughts away, I glanced to Cade again. "Aren't you supposed to be at work?"

He shrugged. "Quiet day. And my crew's not on call."

Amelia asked Holly something about her hospital work schedule and then Janet stopped by the table. It was so good to be home. All of the tension and worry that had been knotted like a vise around my chest eased when I was surrounded by friends and family like this.

———

A few days later, I stopped by Willow Brook Fire & Rescue. I was there to pick up a set of car keys from Cade. He'd all but ordered me to take his extra truck, insisting it was mine to keep. Considering that I didn't want to keep borrowing my mother's car, I'd decided to take him up on his offer for now.

As I stepped through the front entrance into the station, I couldn't help but wonder if I'd see Caleb. If it hadn't been for the fact that I was staying with my parents, I had to admit I would probably be camped out at his place all the time. He wasn't above trying to cajole me into it either. He'd already done so in a few calls and texts.

The option of having my own vehicle was appealing for more reasons than one. Because, you see, it wasn't that I felt the need to hide what I was doing, but constantly using my mother's car to see Caleb... well, she would probably be ecstatic about it, and I had some dignity.

Being home, I was starting to feel more relaxed than I had

in years. Truth be told, a huge part of it was the fact I didn't have my phone. Caleb had point blank told me he wouldn't be letting me know when texts from Lance showed up. Now that it was all out in the open with everyone, the shame around it was starting to fade. Shame wasn't a rational feeling, yet it had held me back from being open about this earlier. I kept replaying everything in the lead up to when it all started and wondering if I'd done something wrong to provoke Lance.

Cade and Amelia had stopped by for dinner at our parents' house the other night as well when he and my father discussed the whole mess. Between my dad and Caleb, I was starting to have sprouts of hope that perhaps somehow they'd be able to stop Lance once and for all, so I could find some peace.

As the door to the station fell closed behind me, I looked up to see a woman I didn't recognize. I knew of her, if only because she'd become legendary in small-town Willow Brook for stealing Beck Steele's heart. Maisie Steele was Carol Rogers' granddaughter. She'd not only inherited her grandmothers old home, but she stepped right into her shoes as the main dispatcher for Willow Brook Fire & Rescue. Rumor had it that Beck, teasingly known when I was younger as a flirt extraordinaire, had fallen head over heels in love with her. They'd since married and had one baby with another one on the way.

"You must be Maisie," I said as I approached the reception counter, taking in her riot of dark brown curls and wide brown eyes. Her eyelashes were so thick, I could see them curling against her cheeks from where I stood several feet away. She was absolutely adorable. She looked slightly puzzled when she glanced up, so I clarified. "I'm Ella Masters, Cade's sister."

A wide smile stretched across Maisie's face. "Oh wow! Everybody is so happy you moved home, so I am too and I don't even know you! I feel like I do though," she said as she stepped around from the counter, pulling me into a hug and startling the hell out of me.

When she stepped back and saw the look on my face, she shrugged sheepishly. "I'm good friends with Amelia and Lucy, so by extension your brother too."

"Of course," I replied. "It's so nice to meet you. If you didn't know it, you're legendary."

Maisie cocked her head to the side, her gaze puzzled. "Legendary?"

"Uh huh. Nobody expected Beck Steele to fall in love with anyone. But rumor has it, he fell for you pretty damn quick."

Maisie's cheeks flushed. As if conjured by name, the door to the side of the reception area opened, and Beck himself walked through. Though I was a few years younger than Beck, I knew him quite well. He'd been a friend of Cade's growing up here in Willow Brook. "Ella!" Beck walked to me and pulled me into a quick hug.

Stepping back, I glanced up and grinned. "Hey Beck, long time, no see."

He didn't appear to hear me as he was busy dropping a kiss in the curve of Maisie's neck. The amount of love in his gaze was powerful enough to make my own heart give a thump, if only for being witness to it. Beck had always been a nice guy, yet a relentless flirt. It was good to see him so happy.

"So I hear you're a father now," I commented when he straightened and leaned his elbow on the reception counter.

Beck smiled widely, running a hand through his black curls, his green eyes crinkling at the corners. "You heard right. Max is the best baby in the universe. I love being a dad. Plus, I think I'm great at it," he said, casting a teasing grin to Maisie.

She chuckled softly. "You are except when you're spoiling him rotten."

Beck shrugged affably. "Except then. So I hear you're here to stay. Is that so?" he asked, shifting gears.

"That's the plan," I offered with a nod.

The door to the back opened again, and this time Cade walked through. He had a set of keys in his hands, which he tossed in my direction when he saw me. Catching them, I arched a brow. "You sure about this?"

Cade leaned his elbow against the reception counter beside Beck, while Maisie rounded the counter to answer an incoming call.

"Do we have to have this conversation again?" Cade asked.

I bit the inside of my cheek and shrugged. "I suppose not. It just seems like kind of a big thing to give me."

"It's an old truck," Cade said flatly, as if that explained everything. "I changed the oil and made sure everything was up to speed, but it's nothing special. It's the old beater I still had hanging around from high school. Amelia will give me hell if I try to bring it back home at this point, so you'd better take it. She's sick of it sitting in the driveway."

"All right, all right," I said, sliding the keys in my pocket.

Beck's cell phone rang, and he stepped away, giving me a wave as he pushed through the door into the back again.

"Anything new?" Cade asked.

"Nope. I need to find a place to stay next, but I've got time."

Cade's eyes narrowed, and I sensed the direction he was going. Holding a hand up, I shook my head. "You don't need to warn me. Mom and Dad have already made it clear they want me to stay with them until everything blows over with Lance. But I'm fine. It's been going on for over a year and a half. Plus, it's not like a place to stay will pop up anytime soon. It's Willow Brook, and we're headed into winter. I love Mom and Dad, but now Dad's more worried than he ever was, and Mom is hovering. You know how I feel about that."

Cade ran a hand through his hair with a sigh. "They're just worried about you, Ella. I get it, but..."

I shook my head. "No you don't. You're the big brother. They never worried about you the way they did me. Then with the accident, that just made it worse."

Cade pushed away from the counter, stepping in front of me and glancing down. "Okay, no use in arguing about this. It's good to have you home, sis. I gotta go though. I promised Amelia I'd be home soon. Speaking of that, she wants to have you out for dinner. When can you come?"

"It's safe to say my schedule's flexible," I said with a laugh. Which was quite true. Although I was getting busy with my new job, I was discovering that working from home on research and writing papers was a good fit for me. I was an early bird and preferred to get up at the crack of dawn. I was usually done with my work for the day by early afternoon.

Cade nodded as he stepped back. "I'll check with Amelia and text you. Caleb's number, right?"

At my nod, he waved and walked out. Maisie was finishing a call, and I was suddenly at loose ends. I'd barely allowed myself to think much about it, but I'd been hoping I would run into Caleb here.

As if my thoughts alone conjured him, the next person who came through the door from the back was Caleb. He was looking down at what I presumed to be my phone as he walked through, so he didn't see me right away. His eyes narrowed, and a flash of anxiety coiled in my gut.

But then he looked up, his eyes landing on me. He immediately put the phone away in his pocket and flashed a grin.

"Anything I need to worry about?" I asked when he stopped in front of me.

He shook his head quickly. "No, not at all."

"Are you sure? Because..."

Caleb shook his head again, more forcefully this time.

"Not much point in me having your phone if you're gonna ask for updates about it all the time."

Warmth curled around my heart. Part of me wanted to push back against how much I savored his protectiveness, but it felt too good right this second for me to dwell on it.

Sweet hell, he looked so good too. His dark brown hair was damp, and I presumed he'd just showered. It was approaching evening. His espresso gaze coasted over me, lighting little fires under my skin everywhere it landed.

I'd been trying to convince myself that I didn't want him as desperately as I did, but it was pointless. Ever since the other night, which was now three days ago, I'd barely been able to stop thinking about him. He texted me regularly, but he'd been busy with two fires, including one that took him out of town overnight.

I was also still trying to get my footing under me here, and though I certainly didn't need to answer to my parents about my choices, it was rather awkward to sashay away to see Caleb every night. That was a big part of the reason I wanted to find a way to move out sooner rather than later. That and the fact that my mother's tendency to hover would drive me to the edge of crazy pretty soon.

As I stood there, simply staring at him, he spoke, voicing my own thoughts aloud. "I miss you. Come home with me tonight."

His confidence was intoxicating as was the depth and honesty of his desire for me. I was nodding before my brain had formed a thought. His mouth curled up at one corner in a slow grin. My belly promptly executed a flip.

I'd forgotten how it felt to feel like this. Joy had been scarce for me in the last ten years. Getting through to the other side of the accident had sucked the joy right out of my life. Trying to avoid facing my grief had only dragged it out. When I finally thought I had found my footing again, it had been ruined so quickly. It wasn't that I'd purposefully not dated anyone once Lance started pulling his shit, but I simply hadn't been interested. It had made me uncomfortable to even think about myself like that.

Yet, right here, right now, with Caleb, joy bubbled up inside, tangling with a carefree, thrumming desire.

"I have a truck," I said, tugging the keys out of my pocket and holding them up.

When Caleb arched a brow, I continued. "Cade insisted I take his old truck. This way, I don't have to rely on my mom so much anymore."

Caleb nodded, his eyes flicking up to my hairline. Lifting his hand, he traced his fingers over the freshly healing scar. "How does it feel?"

"Fine. It wasn't too bad, but then you knew that."

I didn't voice the jumble of emotions crowding my heart. He made me feel so protected, so cared for. Every small gesture sent another curl of warmth around my heart. Why, oh why, had I avoided this for so long?

His finger slid down, tucking a lock of hair behind my ear and sending a shiver through me. The moment felt so intimate, and he'd barely touched me.

So absorbed in the moment, I completely forgot we had an audience with Maisie only a few feet away. She audibly cleared her throat, and my cheeks flushed hot as I glanced sideways.

She smiled brightly at both of us. "So what are you guys going to have for dinner then?" she asked.

She giggled when Caleb shook his head slowly. "Hey, I've been here the whole time. But apparently, you two totally forgot. I'm all for it though. By the way,"—she paused, casting her eyes to me—"Caleb isn't a very good cook. At least, that's what the guys say. When they're out in the field, no one lets him cook."

Her teasing snapped me out of my embarrassment, and I laughed. "He's not, but I'll make something. Come on, we'll go to the store first."

Chapter Fifteen

CALEB

I leaned my elbows on the counter and watched while Ella finished putting the dishes in the dishwasher. I'd offered to do most of the cleanup, but she'd swatted me away. I took a pull on my beer, savoring the sight of her as she bent over to put the last plate in the bottom rack. I'd conveniently forgotten what a sweet ass she had. Well, it wasn't that I'd forgotten, it was that she'd filled out more, so it was even sweeter than I remembered.

It was a good thing my memories hadn't been that sharp. If they had, the blade of missing her would've sliced deeper. It had cut deep enough as it was.

When she straightened and turned around, her hair fell loose from the knot atop her head. The rich brown locks tumbled in a graceful swing, cascading down her back. Her cheeks were flushed, her lips pink, and her green eyes bright in the dim light. I was trying to be a gentleman and not just fuck her senseless the moment I saw her. Yet, my restraint was taking its toll.

My cock had been straining against my jeans for most of the evening. The simple fact of her existence, of *finally* having her back here, had only served to refresh my memories of how much she meant to me. There had *never* been a woman who called to me the way Ella did. The attraction between us was raw, a power of its own—she was a magnet whose force I could not resist. Mingling in with that was a sense of protectiveness to the point that I felt half insane. Lance, who was just a number on her phone, had sent another series of texts earlier today while I'd been out responding to a local fire.

It was a damn good thing I made a habit of leaving my phone at the station when I was on duty. Our crew had been called out to a minor fire in the kitchen at a hunting cabin. Nothing major, it was all in a days work for us, but I'd have lost my focus if I'd seen those messages while I was out.

After I'd returned to the station and seen the messages after my shower, I'd wanted to pummel the fucking guy, and he was nowhere near here. So all I'd done was as Rex requested and simply forwarded them to him with a quick text asking for him to give me a call soon. I hoped like hell he had some updates on the situation.

The fury I felt at seeing those texts and knowing she'd been seeing them for too damn long amplified everything I felt. So with her standing there by the counter, her cheeks flushed and her hair in a tousle around her shoulders, my restraint was at the end of its tether, about to snap.

I wasn't much for trying to take this slow, so I didn't even bother. Setting my beer down and rounding the island between us, I reached out, catching Ella's hand in mine and reeling her to me. I savored her soft gasp as her body bumped against mine. I didn't care that my arousal was obvious, I didn't care about anything but this moment and getting as close as physically possible to her.

Her gaze darkened as she looked up at me, her tongue darting out to moisten her lips. I meant to say something, but I didn't. I was done for the moment her tongue swiped across her bottom lip.

Releasing her hand, I brushed a loose lock of hair out of her eyes and fit my mouth over hers. On her gasp, I swept my tongue into the sweet welcome of her mouth. Inside of a hot second, I was lost, devouring her mouth with deep sweeps of my tongue, nips on her bottom lip, and rocking my hips into the cradle of hers. Sliding my palm free of her hair, I swept it down her back to cup her lush bottom, palming it and rocking my arousal into her.

It might've been a distant memory before the other night, but it was sharp and vivid now — the way she came alive and let go once the heat of our desire engulfed us. In high school, I'd had a thing for her for a bit before we were together. I'd loved the contrast of how serious and quiet she could be, always a straight-A student, always on the honor roll and always more focused on her studies than anything else. I still remembered the first time I kissed her. Just like now there'd been a moment of hesitation and then it swept away in the fire that flashed hot and high between us.

With her tongue tangling with mine and her hands reaching around to grab my ass, our kiss went wild. I couldn't get enough of her fast enough. I wasn't thinking, everything was pure raw sensation. Tugging at her clothes, I was relieved she was wearing a blouse even though she swore at me when I tore a button loose.

"Take it easy," she murmured.

Dragging my tongue down her neck and savoring the sweet tangy taste, I reluctantly lifted my head. "Easy for you to say," I muttered, canting my eyes to the side and back to her.

My T-shirt had gotten caught on a knife handle in the dish rack when she yanked it over my head and tossed it aside. It was still dangling there. Ella giggled, her cheeks flushing a deeper shade of pink. A sly grin curled the corners of her lips.

Unbuttoning her jeans, I shoved them swiftly down over her hips. She was quite the multi-tasker, busy trying to tug at mine at the same time. She wobbled with another giggle when she kicked her feet free from her jeans.

Lifting her, I slid her hips on the counter, taking a moment to absorb the sight of her. Her lips were swollen from our kisses, her eyes dark, reflecting that same wild, intense, almost frantic need I knew was held in my gaze. Her hair was a tangled mess, falling down over her shoulders and partially masking her breasts.

Leaning forward, I laved my tongue over the black silk, scoring her nipple lightly with my teeth and dampening the silk. I did the same to the other, savoring her cries as she arched into me. With a flick of my thumb on the clasp between her breasts, her breasts tumbled loose. I savored the weight of them in my palms as I glanced up to meet her wild gaze.

"Not fair," she muttered as she reached between us and tore at the buttons on my fly. When her palm curled over the length of my cock through the thin cotton of my briefs, I couldn't hold back a groan.

I needed more hands than I had. I didn't want to let go of the feel of her breasts in my palms, her nipples taut as I teased them with my thumbs. But, just as much, I needed to feel the core of her. Reluctantly, I released her breasts, trailing my fingers down over the soft curve of her belly and dragging them across the wet silk between her thighs. She was drenched.

"Fuck Ella. You make me crazy. You're so fucking wet."

I didn't think it was physically possible, but my cock swelled even more. Just at the knowledge of how wet she was for me.

Thought fled again, what little grasp I had on it for a few seconds there. I needed her bare, completely bare. Hooking my thumb on the thin strip of silk on her hip, I lifted her hips with my other hand, yanking her panties down her legs. She kicked them free, the silk falling softly to the floor. Meanwhile, she was tearing my fly open and pushing my briefs out of the way. My cock sprang free, and I groaned when she curled her palm around it.

Much as I wanted to sink inside of her right away, more than that I needed to taste her. Yanking her hips to the edge of the counter, I leaned over, teasing a nipple with my tongue, dusting kisses over her belly and sinking my fingers into the warm silky wet clench of her core.

Her hands tunneled into my hair, gripping it as I dragged my tongue across her seam. She tasted so good—salty with a hint of sweetness and all Ella. Fucking her slowly with my fingers, I explored every inch of her folds, teasing over her clit again and again while she gripped my hair and chanted my name in between gasps and cries. I could feel her getting closer and closer to the edge. I buried my fingers inside of her, knuckle deep, and caught her clit with my teeth. Her channel gripped my fingers when she cried out, flying apart. I waited until her hips stopped rocking before drawing back. Straightening, I soaked her in—her eyes hazy with passion and her shoulders curling towards me as she caught her breath.

Her lips were parted, her breath coming in little gasps. Lifting a hand, I brushed her hair back from her face, dragging my thumb across her bottom lip. Her tongue darted out, and she caught it in her teeth, sucking it lightly.

Fuck me. Ella owned me—body, heart and soul. Just that tiny motion, and my cock swelled so hard it ached. I needed to be inside of her. Shifting, I shoved my briefs down over my hips, too hurried to even bother getting out of my jeans. Glancing up at her, I curled my fist around my cock. Only then did reality hit me.

"Fuck. Condom," I muttered as I pushed back. I was going to have to walk all the way upstairs to deal with this issue.

Ella caught my hips with her legs, pulling me back close to her. "I'm on the pill," she murmured. "And I'm clean. I know you must be too."

I stared at her for a long moment, my mind spinning back years. Back in high school, we'd never had sex without a condom. My father had put the fear of God in me about that. But I was older now and so was she, and I didn't doubt she was on the pill.

This was her call though, not mine. "Are you sure?"

She nodded emphatically. On the heels of a deep breath, I stepped back to her again, gripping her hips and sliding her all the way to the edge of the counter. Adjusting the angle of my hips, I sank inside of her creamy clench in one swift surge.

She cried out, her hips rocking into me instantly. I wanted to drag this out, to make it slow, to savor every second of it. But the intensity was too much, my need too great, and the years of missing her carrying so much weight that all I could do was lose myself inside of her. I rocked into her again and again, murmuring her name over and over as heat and pleasure twisted at my spine. I felt her channel throbbing around me. Reaching between us, I swirled my thumb over her clit, opening my eyes to witness her cry out, her body arching back and going taut, clamping down around my cock.

Only then did I let go, the heat twisting at the base of my spine and slamming through me, my release pouring into her with one last surge.

Chapter Sixteen

ELLA

Caleb called my name as his head fell into the dip of my shoulder. I felt the shudders of his body while tremors of pleasure were still wracking mine. My skin was damp, and I could hardly catch my breath, gulping in air as I came down from the intensity of my climax crashing through me.

His palms slid down my sides to rest at the curve of my waist. The tile counter was cool against my skin, a contrast to the heat inside and out. It was heaven to feel him so close to me. I savored the hard planes of his body and the feel of his strength encompassing me.

When I felt him lift his head, I dragged my eyes open to find his waiting. My heart twisted sharply inside my chest. Everything felt so intense. It was so easy to simply lose myself in him, in the heat of our desire, in the heartbeat of every moment.

We stared at each other, intimacy shimmering around us, hazy in the air. Again just as before, it felt as if time was falling away. I was simultaneously falling backwards and barreling forward. I would wonder later if everything felt so heightened with him because of how much I'd had to shut myself down to get through the last year and a half. But for now, I felt free of those worries and let them fall away.

I felt the subtle, prickly sensation of his thumb brushing across my scarred skin, crossing over to the smooth surface of my unblemished skin. The contrast in sensation was odd and something I hadn't felt often. I couldn't help but love that Caleb didn't even seem to notice the scars, not in a way where he was careful, or as if he had to be aware of them.

There was a thump behind us and then Caleb's mouth curled in a grin as his eyes flicked beyond my shoulder. "Looks like we have company," he observed.

Creamsicle leapt onto the counter, keeping a safe distance away, his tail twitching back and forth. I'd had a cat when I was a little girl, but I'd forgotten how inquisitive they could be. Creamsicle's amber eyes surveyed us. After another moment, he turned away, leaping to the floor and heading over to his seat on the windowsill.

I bit my lip as I glanced up at Caleb. "I suppose..."

Before I had a chance to finish whatever I meant to say, which probably wasn't sensible, Caleb lifted me against him and carried me upstairs. It was late, the lingering rays of the late autumn sun leaving nothing but a burst of orange, gold and red in the sky.

The view from his bedroom was spectacular. The mountain ridge in the distance was outlined against the darkening sky as the inky night took over. Once he reached the foot of his bed, he eased me down, only then pulling out of me. I instantly missed the feel of him filling me, if only because it was the closest we could possibly be. And right about now, the feeling of intimacy and complete safety that I felt when I was tangled up with Caleb, well, I would just about sell my soul to keep feeling it.

His bed was luxurious with pillows piled high, cool sheets and a lightweight down comforter. The air gusted across my skin as he lifted the comforter and let it fall over us, pulling me close against his side as my skin prickled at the chill chasing over me.

"You didn't even ask me if I wanted to stay," I teased.

His eyes canted down to meet mine, a gleam visible in the fading light. "Do I need to ask?"

I shook my head against his shoulder, tracing circles on his chest with my fingertip. "No."

"Okay then," he murmured, dusting a kiss on my hairline, just below where my new scar was.

I tumbled into a deep sleep. I could've gotten addicted to this. Falling asleep with Caleb was a heaven I hadn't contemplated. I wasn't much for cuddling, or so I'd thought. In the few dating relationships I'd had after high school and before the last year and a half when everything went to hell, spending the night had always been more of an afterthought and nothing I thought too much about.

Yet with Caleb, it appeared I was a cuddler. Though we'd always been affectionate when we were dating in high school, I'd never spent the night with him. Because, well, we were in high school. He'd tried to cajole me into it, but the downside to having a father who was the police chief in town was trying to sneak around for anything seemed impossible. Oh, we'd had sex, in fact I lost my virginity to him. But we'd never spent the night together. I couldn't have known that he would hold me close all night—pulling me up against his side where I could comfortably drape myself over him, or spooning behind me, holding me in the cage of his arms.

That was how I woke the following day—with the sun angling across the bed and Caleb's warm, hard body curled behind me. His palm rested on the curve of my belly, and I could feel his breath rise and fall, slow and steady, against my back.

I shifted my hips, my body reflexively seeking to be closer, and felt his quite obvious arousal against my bottom. I was instantly slick between my thighs. My body moved on its own accord, my hips shifting restlessly, trying to ease the ache at my core. I felt him come awake from a subtle shift in his breathing. He murmured something and then flexed in a shivering stretch that I felt to my bones.

His palm slid up my belly to cup one of my breasts. My nipples puckered, instantly tight and achy. "Mmm, Ella," he murmured in my hair before dropping a kiss against my shoulder. He was warm all over, and I loved it. I tended to be cold. All the damn time.

Much as I loved winter and I loved Alaska, I had never loved the cold that came with it. I was the kind of person who went to sleep with socks on just to keep my feet warm. That wasn't necessary with Caleb. He was my own personal heater.

My hips shifted back against him again. I couldn't resist rocking into the hard, hot length of him. Because I knew what I wanted and where I wanted it. I turned my head, reaching a hand up to trace along the strong line of his jaw. He caught my lips in a kiss.

On the heels of a breath, his hand slid down, sifting through the curls at the apex of my thighs and dipping his fingers into my folds.

"Fuck Ella, you're so wet already.

I rocked into his touch as he teased me with his fingers for a moment. He didn't make me wait. He shifted, lifting my leg over his calf and sinking into me from behind, burying himself to the hilt.

He held still for a beat, brushing the hair back from my neck and dragging his tongue in a blazing path over my skin, his thumb tracing my lips before I turned. Another hot wet kiss, and then we rocked together, the motion languid and slow. Still sleepy, it felt like a dream—one where I was caught in a shimmering web of intimacy with him. Nothing existed outside of us together. Sensation unspooling inside, I was at the edge inside of a few seconds, murmuring his name. His hand slid down over my belly again, dipping into my curls and teasing over my clit.

My climax unraveled, everything in me fracturing apart in slow motion as pleasure rocked me deeply. I felt his release as he went taut above me for a moment before he shuddered. We lay still, our breath coming in soft heaves together.

As my brain flickered back online, I thought to myself that I couldn't believe this was happening. I couldn't believe I was here.

Yet again, time collapsed. I hadn't felt this way since before the accident. And yet, this was even more intense. As if I'd finally made it to the other side of the lingering grief and guilt. As if we'd somehow earned this by walking through fire. The burn of the pain was something else altogether now.

———

A little while later after we showered and dressed, I glanced across the counter at Caleb as he pushed his plate back. I'd gotten ingredients for pancakes when we went to the store last night. It was all rather domestic. While I didn't quite know what to think of any of it because it was racing at me so fast, it felt so good, so right that I couldn't stop it.

The easy feeling was shattered when a phone started buzzing—again and again and again. My gut coiled with dread, and I felt sick instantly.

Chapter Seventeen

CALEB

The phone vibrated over on the table by the door where I left it last night—again, again, and again. Ella's eyes darkened and fear flashed through them. Her features tensed, and that was all it took to make me furious. Not with her. Rather, over the fucking asshole who'd been tugging on the strings of her peace of mind like this.

I spun away from the counter, walking swiftly toward the door and snatching the phone. I didn't even look at the messages. I just turned the phone off. Because I'd be damned if I'd let that asshole reach across space and time and ruin this morning.

Ella was right behind me, reaching for the phone. "What did they say?"

"Ella, it doesn't matter. I'm sure you can imagine. Leave it alone. Talk to your dad today. He's got some feelers out on this to see what he can do."

Her lips tightened as she looked at me, her cheeks flushing, but not in a good way.

Spinning back around, she walked to the windows, crossing her arms tightly. "I know you're trying to help," she finally said. "But I don't like this feeling. I don't need you to take over like this. I don't need my dad to take over."

I bit back the curse that wanted to fly out of my mouth.

Walking to stand beside her, I stared out over the view. Mist was rising off of the field in front of the house. It had been cool enough last night to leave a light dusting of frost on everything. As the sun's rays angled across the landscape, mist rose in the air with the frost evaporating. A misty view of the sunrise stretched out in front of us.

"Ella, no one's trying to take over. I don't want you to have to deal with that shit. Neither does your dad."

She glanced up at me, nothing but frustration staring back at me in her gaze. I had to admit, I didn't understand why it would bother her to have us try to shield her from this. But it clearly did.

"It's not that I don't want help, but I'm not helpless. I don't..." she sighed, shaking her head. "I can't explain it. I want help but I don't want help. That's all."

Staring down at her, my heart twisted sharply in my chest. I understood what she meant. Yet, all I wanted to do was shield her from all of this. Uncertain what to say to ease her mind, I simply nodded. I pulled her close, feeling the tension in her body. After a moment, she relaxed. But we didn't speak of it again.

———

Later the following day, I sank into the chair across from Rex's desk. In the last day or so, the text messages had picked up the pace. I'd been forwarding them to Rex. The theme was just like the first messages I'd seen—an undertone of threatening, telling her he wouldn't stop, telling her he'd find her, telling her she couldn't escape, on and on.

Staring at Rex, I sighed. "Please tell me there's something you can do about this. I can't believe this bullshit."

Rex mirrored my sigh, raking a hand through his salt and

pepper hair. "Here's the thing with assholes like that. Now's the time when things pick up. Because she's removed herself from any proximity to him. He was getting off on rattling her and shaking her up without every laying a hand on her. Now, he can't see her so he doesn't get the satisfaction of knowing he's fucking with her. So he's going to amp it up."

"Yeah, but is he actually going to come up here? I'll be honest, it might be fucking crazy but part of me wishes he would. Because I'll beat the shit out of him."

Rex narrowed his eyes. "You know damn well that's a bad idea. If he dared to come up here, I'd be able to do something about it. They sent up his records from Portland, and I ran his background check. No surprise, but this isn't the first time he's done this. He was charged and convicted in Washington State for doing the same thing to a colleague there. Clearly, this is his MO. It sucks, but it tells me he'll probably back off after a little bit. Doesn't change the fact that I want him to face charges again one way or another. He got too ballsy in Washington and tried to break into the woman's house. So, while he didn't face any charges for harassing texts and emails, or anything at work, he got slapped with breaking and entering charges. Worked out a plea deal and didn't do any time since he had a clean record before that. My guess is he moved to another state because misdemeanor charges don't pop up in different states, only felonies. The bullshit he pulls—the texts and emails—those are like trying to nail jelly to a wall. Especially when they're not doing anything in person."

There was a knock on Rex's office door. Both of us glanced over to see Cade stepping into the office.

"What's going on?" Cade asked, standing in the doorway. Cade and his father looked so damn alike, it was almost amusing. Cade was a younger, less weathered version of his father with the same steady, low-key demeanor, and easygoing attitude.

At Rex's wave, Cade walked to the desk and leaned his

hip on it. Cade and I hadn't spoken much in the last few weeks, but I knew he was aware of me persuading Ella to use a different phone because he'd thanked me for it.

Rex glanced to Cade and shrugged. "Nothing new and nothing that won't piss you off," he offered with a bitter laugh.

"Please tell me this fucker can get charged with something," Cade said, not even bothering to ask what we were talking about.

"Working on it," Rex replied. "I've got my buddy in Anchorage who handles Internet crimes helping me. Those are easier to deal with than the phone stuff. Far as I can tell, he swaps out burner phones for the texting."

I nodded. "Definitely. He uses a different number every time. The tone in the texts is similar, but that's it."

"Don't suppose I want to see them, huh?" Cade asked.

I shook my head slowly. "Oh, I'll show you but it's just gonna piss you off."

At that moment, I heard Ella's voice along with another feminine voice. In a few seconds, she appeared in the doorway with Amelia, Cade's wife.

Cade's expression softened immediately when Amelia stepped to his side and dropped a kiss on his cheek. He slipped his arm casually around her waist, hooking his thumb in the back pocket of her jeans.

Amelia glanced around, casting a smile about the room. "What's up?"

Ella's eyes met mine, and I had to restrain the urge to stand and pull her into my arms. We had an audience, a quite specific audience of her brother and her father.

I made do with a smile. Rex grinned at her. "Ella, good to see you stopping by. What are you two doing here?"

"I asked Ella to meet me here. She's coming to girls' night," Amelia explained, tucking a lock of her amber hair behind her ear. Amelia was tall, almost as tall as Cade. I guessed she was close to six feet tall, seeing as I was barely taller than her at six feet, two inches. She and Cade had dated back in high school, broken up and now were quite happily married. I wouldn't dare say it aloud, but Amelia had just dashed my hopes at another night with Ella.

"Girls' night is here?" Cade asked, a look of mild alarm in his eyes.

Amelia chuckled. "Oh yeah, we're taking over the station." Nudging him with her elbow, she shook her head. "No, I dropped my work truck off for an oil change next door, so I asked Ella to meet me here. I figured it was a good excuse to stop by and see you."

Cade flashed a grin, glancing between Rex and me. "That means we're up for cards at Wildlands tonight. Wanna come?"

Rex shook his head with a smile. "I'm getting too old for that. You guys have fun without me."

"I'll be there," I replied.

Amelia dropped another kiss on Cade's cheek and stepped away. "We'll get going. I'll see you when you get home tonight." Glancing around with a grin, she continued, "He'll be worried about coming home to tipsy women. Come on Ella, let's go. If you need a ride tonight, you can stay at our place."

I bit back the urge to offer to pick Ella up. I didn't need our audience of overprotective family members to wonder what that meant, especially when my intentions were anything but pure.

Rex called to Ella as she started to turn away. "You're still forwarding me your emails, right?"

She turned back, a look of subtle annoyance flashing across her face. "Of course. I haven't gotten any recently. Why are you asking?"

I wisely held my tongue because I'd already had a taste of her irritation on this topic. Cade, on the other hand, didn't even bother to hold back. "Because that fucking asshole is still texting. Please don't shut anybody out on this. This is serious."

Ella went from annoyed to *really* annoyed. Resting a hand on her hip, her eyes narrowed. "You don't need to boss me around. I know it's serious. I've been dealing with it for over a year and a half."

With a roll of her eyes and a shake of her head, she spun around, stalking out of the room. At the last minute, she called over her shoulder. "I'm an adult you know, not your kid sister anymore."

Amelia had stayed quiet. Glancing to Cade, she sighed. "I know you're worried, but don't get all high-handed about it. It won't help."

Cade ran a hand through his hair with a ragged sigh, glancing between Rex and me. Before he had a chance to speak, Amelia added, "It's not that I don't understand. I'm just saying, don't let her feel like you're taking over everything. That would annoy me, and it'll definitely annoy her. I know you're worried. Just back off a little." She paused and caught his hand in hers, giving it a squeeze before she walked out of the room. "See you tonight."

After the sound of their footsteps was beyond earshot, Cade glanced to me and then to his father. "What the fuck? Why is Ella so annoyed about this?"

"Because she likes to take care of things herself. She was always like that. No need to lecture her on it either," Rex said, flicking his eyes between us.

I lifted my hands in mock surrender. "You don't need to tell me. She already got frustrated with me about it this morning too. But she didn't take her phone back, so I'm taking that as a win."

Cade's eyes narrowed, but he didn't say a word. Rex's phone rang, conveniently ending this conversation.

As Cade and I left, walking down the hall over to the fire station side of the building, he paused in the hallway, turning to face me. "This morning?"

I silently groaned. Fuck. I didn't need Ella's overprotective older brother getting on me about her. But, he was her brother, and he was my friend. I couldn't blow him off.

"Don't even start, man. You know how I feel about her."

"Actually, I don't," he said, sliding his hands in the pockets of his jeans and leaning against the wall.

Turning to face him, I glanced around, relieved to see no one else happened to be nearby at the moment. "Dude, I loved her, and I still do. How about you let me have a shot at the chance we never got after the accident?"

Cade was quiet, staring at me for a long, taut moment. He finally nodded, pushing off the wall behind him. "Fair enough. If you..."

I cut him off. "Man, you don't ever have to worry about that with me. You should know that by now. I would never do anything to hurt Ella. My biggest mistake was not fighting harder for us after the accident."

Cade held my gaze for a few beats and then dipped his head. We turned in unison and walked into the break room at the back.

Chapter Eighteen

ELLA

Lucy Phillips threw her cards out on the table and glared at Maisie. "Jesus fucking Christ. Just when I think I have a good enough hand to beat you, you win anyway."

Lucy brushed her blonde hair back from her face and snagged the bottle of wine in the middle of the table, quickly filling her glass to the brim and taking a gulp. I looked down at my hand, which had been decent. Meanwhile, Maisie shrugged and smiled slightly. "I love winning," she said.

Lucy, whose attitude belied her almost fairy-like appearance with her blonde hair, blue eyes and petite frame, narrowed her eyes and shook her head slowly.

"I feel like I'm missing something here," I interjected.

Amelia who sat beside me nudged me with her elbow and laughed. "Maisie usually wins. Despite his many flaws, her dad was a hard core poker player."

Maisie piped in. "Exactly. That's how he made his living for most of my childhood. I know how to play, and I know how to play well. I can't bring myself to throw a game just for the hell of it. We don't have to play cards every week," she offered, glancing over to Lucy who still looked put out by the whole thing.

Susannah chuckled and took a sip of her water. "I think half the fun for Lucy is getting pissed off at you," she offered to Maisie with a wry grin.

I knew Susannah from growing up in Willow Brook. She'd been a few years ahead of me in high school. At the moment, she was very pregnant and due within the next few weeks. With her strawberry blonde hair, her wide blue eyes and fair freckled skin, she was practically glowing. She was a hotshot firefighter and tough as nails. She'd complained tonight about the frustrations of doing nothing but light duty at the station for the last few months.

Lucy cast her glare in Susannah's direction now. "Half the fun isn't me getting pissed off."

Amelia chuckled again. "Sure it is. I work with you every day. You thrive off of getting angry."

Lucy finally burst out laughing. "Okay, fine. I might—just a little—have fun giving you a hard time."

"Okay, so the deal is Maisie wins every week then?" I asked

Amelia shrugged. "Not every week. Every once in a while one of us beats her. I figured you might have a shot. I remembered when we were little Cade used to get annoyed when you beat him at rummy."

"Uh, that was chance. My card skills are completely average," I replied, setting my cards down on the table.

Lucy, promptly proving Amelia's point, picked everyone's cards up, started shuffling and immediately dealt another hand. As the cards were dealt, I glanced around the table. Susannah winced slightly, reaching her hand behind her back to rub it lightly.

Maisie got right to the point. "Are you about to go into labor?"

Susannah shook her head with a laugh. "No, but I wish. I was telling Dr. Jenkins the other day that I can't wait for these last few weeks to be over. I'm sick of feeling like a beached whale. I have to pee all the damn time. She's constantly reminding me I need to stay hydrated when I'd rather not because then I have to pee more. And Ward is driving me fucking insane," she said with a groan.

Maisie burst out laughing. "I'll just bet he is. He doesn't know what to do with himself around the station these days. Beck was laughing about it the other night. That man is so damn whipped."

Susannah smiled softly, but it faded fast. "I love him, but he's a bit much. I'm too uncomfortable to deal with his hovering. I told him I preferred sleeping on the couch, and you should've seen his face. It didn't matter that I like it because it has that reclining section. So then he offered to sleep out there with me on the other side of the sectional."

I glanced to Amelia, wondering if she and Cade were planning to have kids anytime soon. As though she read my mind, she shrugged. "It's a big fat maybe for us. Every time I hear stories like that, I think maybe not."

"Don't worry, she'll have her little baby boy and forget all of it. Then, you'll wonder. Max is already getting big and I miss what he was like when he was younger," Maisie said, referring to her and Beck's son. "I can't believe I'm already pregnant again though." Maisie's eyes landed on me. "What about you and Caleb?"

My cheeks flushed hot, and I glanced over at her, sputtering and then taking a gulp of wine to mask my embarrassment. Maisie winked and caught Amelia's gaze. "It's like I told you. Caleb's ridiculous around her. I might not've known you long," she offered, looking back in my direction "...but Caleb's been at the station for over a year now. He hangs out with the rest of the crews and us. I've never, I mean never, seen him look at a woman the way he looks at you. I'm pretty sure you're it for him."

Lucy smiled slightly. "Perfect. Is it going to be another one of those sappy second chance things? Although you're going to have to work to top Cade and Amelia. I was ready to shake them both by the end of it all."

Glancing to Amelia, I caught her rolling her eyes. Someone kicked my foot, and I looked around. "Oops. That was me. I was aiming for Lucy. Sorry about that," Amelia said.

"I don't know what's going to happen, but I'm so happy you and Cade finally got a clue a few years ago," I said, eager to get the topic off of Caleb and me.

"Slick, aren't you?" Lucy asked with a grin and a wink. "Don't think we didn't miss you trying to change the subject. There's no gossip left about Cade and Amelia. They've been together three years now."

Scanning the table, I saw four expectant pairs of eyes looking back at me. Out of them, I was closest to Amelia, if only because she was my sister-in-law and I'd known her forever. While I knew Susannah, we hadn't been particularly close. Maisie and Lucy were brand new to me.

Yet, I hadn't had a circle of friends like this in Portland. I had a few, but my focus had been so narrow—on academics and on fitting into my job after finishing my doctorate—I hadn't allowed myself much time like this. Even though I was embarrassed and even though this was different, it was nice to relax with their teasing banter.

Amelia spoke, as if sensing my hesitation. "You don't have to talk about you and Caleb. But, like I warned you on the way over here, they're going to ask."

"It's okay," I said, pushing past my embarrassment. "It's just, well..." I looked to Lucy and Maisie, uncertain how much they knew of my history with Caleb. "Things ended on kind of a weird note for us before."

Maisie and Lucy nodded in unison, Lucy speaking first. "We heard about the accident. I mean, you're Cade's sister, and this is a small town. It sounded awful, and I'm sure it was hard."

Maisie was quiet and then she nodded slowly. "I bet it was, but you're here now."

My heart tumbled in my chest. It had taken so, so long for me to get to the point where I could easily talk about that accident. Too long. It was such a relief. I didn't want to dwell on that. Not now. So I addressed their question. "So, well, something's happening. I guess we'll just have to see where it goes."

Blessedly, that seemed to be enough, and conversation moved on. It was fairly late when Levi arrived to pick up Lucy and Maisie, and Ward arrived to pick up Susannah. Levi Phillips was tall and handsome. With his dark blonde hair and blue eyes, he was a contrast to Ward who I hadn't met before. Ward was the superintendent for Caleb's crew. With his almost-black hair and silver eyes, he had a rather intimidating air about him.

The look he gave Susannah was so hot, it was a miracle she didn't catch on fire. Meanwhile, she swatted him away when he tried to help her out of her chair. The tenderness in his gaze made my heart clench. When she was standing with his arm firmly around her waist, he glanced over to me. "Ward," was all he said.

"I'm Ella," I returned. "Cade's sister."

"And Caleb's girl," Levi added. I knew Levi a little bit. He'd moved to Willow Brook with his family while I was still in high school.

He flashed a grin when I glanced over, my eyes widening. "Well, the guy can't shut up about you," he offered with a nonchalant shrug.

Lucy nudged her knee against his leg. "Don't tease her, she's a little sensitive about it."

"Are we ready to go?" he asked with a glance between her and Maisie.

Maisie had carried the empty water and wine glasses over to the sink and turned back. "Sure thing. Beck texted and told me Max is already asleep. I love it when I have girls' night, and I can get home without worrying about putting him to sleep." She looked to Susannah. "Enjoy your last few weeks of sleep," she offered with a wink.

Everyone said their goodbyes and shuffled out with Levi calling over his shoulder to Amelia. "Cade said he'd be here soon. He was helping somebody change a flat tire in the parking lot when we left."

The door slammed shut behind them, and Amelia walked over to the sink, transferring the empty glasses into the dishwasher. The kitchen was quiet, and I leaned back in my chair, taking a deep breath and considering that I should plan to stay here tonight. I'd had a few too many glasses of wine.

"The guestroom is all yours," Amelia said, glancing to me just as there was a knock at the door. Her eyes caught mine again, her brow knitting in confusion.

"Come in," she called. Looking to me, she shrugged. "Cade doesn't knock, so I don't know who the hell this is."

When the door opened, Caleb stepped through. "Levi texted me he didn't have room to take three of you home, so I thought I'd stop and see if you needed a ride."

Amelia looked from me to Caleb and then smiled brightly. "I'm sure she does."

I knew he was stone cold sober if he was here to give me a ride, and I knew exactly what I wanted. I stood and carried my empty wine glass over to Amelia. She rinsed it quickly and set it in the dishwasher before giving me a quick hug. Stepping back, she smiled. "Let's have dinner next Wednesday." She glanced to Caleb. "You're welcome to come too."

My head was nodding along without even thinking. It was so nice to be back where I could see her and Cade regularly. "Of course. Thanks for tonight."

Amelia flashed a wry grin. "Now you'll be expected whenever we get together."

She waved us out. I heard Caleb say goodbye and then felt his presence behind me as I stepped through the door. It was cool and damp out tonight. It had rained this afternoon, but the sky was clear now. The air held an earthy, woodsy scent I associated with autumn.

I paused at the foot of the stairs leading down from the small deck. Taking a deep breath, I leaned my head back to look up into the night. The stars glittered above with wispy clouds moving slowly across the sky. A half moon was rising behind the mountain ridge in the distance as I looked forward again. I took another deep breath and let it out, glancing to Caleb. He didn't say a word. He simply caught my hand in his, and we walked to his truck.

Chapter Nineteen

CALEB

I hadn't wanted to let go of Ella's hand in the car, but by sheer practicality, it had been necessary to start my truck. She was quiet as I drove through the falling darkness, my hand resting on her thigh with our pinkies hooked together.

Nothing could've stopped me from coming to pick her up tonight. Another run of messages from Lance had fired me up. I was furious with him, annoyed with the delays in getting him charged, or whatever the fuck they were going to do. As far as my feelings for Ella though, the more I worried about her and the effect it had on her, the more my heart twisted sharply with the knowledge of how much she meant to me and always had.

I'd boxed my feelings away for her because I'd thought I had no other choice. Now she was back, here to stay, and I'd be damned if I let this chance slip through my fingers again. I was also determined to wipe that haunted look out of her eyes for once and for all.

I rolled my truck to a stop in front of my house, glancing over to see Ella asleep. Though her pinky was still hooked through mine, her head was dipping down to her shoulder. I eased my hand free of hers and climbed quietly out of the truck. Bundling her into my arms, I moved carefully in the hopes that I didn't wake her. I needn't have worried. She was sound asleep, her breath coming soft and steady as I carried her up the stairs.

I stripped her down to her underwear, my cock reacting to the sight of her breasts and the flare of her hips. *Not tonight.* She was out like a light, and I'd be more than content to simply sleep beside her. Climbing into bed with her, I pulled her close against me and tumbled into sleep.

———

I came awake in the darkness. I had to piss like nobody's business, but I didn't want to move. At all. Not with Ella's warm, lush body curled up against me. I sifted my fingers through her hair where her head rested on my shoulder, wishing I didn't need to untangle myself. But nature called.

I moved slowly, sliding out from under her leg thrown over mine and easing her head on the pillow. Taking care of matters quickly, I returned to the bed. I was relieved when she instantly shifted, curling up against my side again. I glanced at the clock to see it was only three in the morning before I fell back into a deep sleep.

The next time I woke, it was to the feel of Ella's hands traveling down over my abs and her lips following them. Though my mind was barely online, my body was in the thick of it. I groaned at the feel of her palm curling around my cock. I heard myself murmuring her name, my breath coming out on another groan as she dragged her tongue from the base of my cock to the tip.

Darkness had shifted to light, the silvery rays of the early sun angling through the windows just above the mountains. Ella was shrouded by the comforter, and I needed to see her. I slid it down, managing to lift my head just as she lifted hers. Her dark brown hair was a tousled mess, her cheeks were flushed, and her eyes bright green with a hint of mischief in them.

"Good morning, Caleb," she murmured, her tongue darting out for another swipe at my cock.

I meant to say something, but my words were lost in a groan when she swirled her tongue around the head of my cock, swiping up a drop of pre-cum. I meant to watch this, to enjoy the sight of it, but lust was lashing at me and sensation was barreling through me. When her eyes fell closed, and she leaned over, drawing me into the warm suction of her mouth, my head fell back against the pillows. I buried my hands in her hair and hung on as she proceeded to drive me completely wild.

She teased me with her tongue, her loose fist gripping my cock. Just when I thought she was going to give me more, she drew back again, her tongue sliding up and down each side of my cock and teasing my balls, which were drawn tight and on the edge of release the whole time.

I lost sight of everything, my focus narrowed to nothing but sensation. By the time she drew me back into her mouth, I was on the verge of exploding. But that wasn't what I wanted. Not just yet. I snatched onto a thread of control, tightening my grip and groaning her name. Lifting my head took immense effort, but I managed it and was rewarded with the sight of her swiping her tongue along her lips.

"Come here," I murmured.

She shook her head, a sly smile stretching across her face.

"Please." I wasn't above begging. "I need to be inside you," I said bluntly.

She stared at me, the air nearly vibrating between us. After a moment, she rose up. "Okay. If that's what you want," she said, her voice husky.

Then, she was straddling me and easing down over me. She teased me some more, her wet pussy sliding back and forth over my cock. Much as I wanted to take the reins—as it was I was at the end of my tether—I sensed she wanted to hold onto the control now. Then, she was rising up, adjusting the angle of my cock and sheathing me. She took me into her, inch by devastating inch, until I was buried deep in the core of her—hot, wet, tight, and pulsing around me.

Chapter Twenty

ELLA

A wave of emotion rocked me as I looked down at Caleb. He filled and stretched me, the feeling so delicious it sent a shiver through me, every fiber of my being humming at the sense of our connection. My hands rested on his chest, nothing but muscle. His hands rested on my hips. His dark chocolate gaze was on mine, the look there so intent I could hardly bear it. I didn't quite know what to make of how quickly I was tumbling into this, but I couldn't look away.

His hands slid up my sides to cup my breasts, teasing my nipples. They were puckered so tight, they ached. The subtle brush of his thumbs across them made me cry out, arching into his touch. I couldn't hold back anymore and I rose up along the length of his cock and back down. His hands eased along my sides again, gripping me just above the curve of my hips.

He didn't even hesitate to touch over the area that was nothing but scar tissue. Tears pricked at my eyes with sensation, need, and emotion colliding together in a storm inside of me. The intensity ran so deep that I tumbled into it, caught in the tornado of everything between us.

Caleb flexed into me, his hips arching up as I rocked into him again and again. Every surge of him filled me deeper, and then he slid one hand free, pressing his thumb over my clit. Sensation gathered, coiling tightly inside. With another press of his thumb, I flew apart, pleasure splintering through me like shards.

I cried out, his name a chant on my lips. I felt the heat of his release inside of me as he went taut when my channel clenched around him. Curling over into his arms, I didn't realize I was crying until I felt the moisture on my cheek against his skin. I rested on him, my breath coming in gasps. I didn't want to talk right now, and I was relieved he didn't try. His palm slid in slow passes up and down my spine.

I didn't know how long we lay still there until I felt him tug the covers up over my back. My skin prickled against the cool cotton sheets. Yet within seconds, I was warm again.

I finally lifted my head, the sense of emotional overwhelm fading. Resting my chin on his chest, I looked at him —his mussed brown hair, the strong lines of his face. As if he sensed my gaze, he opened his eyes. For a moment, his gaze was somber. He lifted a hand, brushing my tangled hair away from my eyes and smoothing it down my back.

"Your hair is so long now," he murmured.

I was relieved at his casual comment. I knew that he knew I'd been crying. But I wasn't up for talking about it just now, because what would I say? There weren't words to attach to what I was feeling—simply that it was all so much.

"It is. Sometimes I think about cutting it again," I replied.

He shook his head quickly. "Please don't."

I laughed softly. "I wasn't planning on it. That's why it's long. When I had it shorter, I needed to get it cut more often, and it was just one more thing to deal with. You know me. I'm not much for dealing with things like hair and make up."

His mouth hitched up at one corner in a grin, and my

belly did a little flip, flutters twirling inside. Just a look from him, nothing more, and it barely mattered we'd just had crazy hot sex first thing in the morning. Because I could've done it all over again.

"I do know you," he murmured, his gravelly voice sending a prickle up my spine as he sifted his fingers through my hair. "You never were one for make up. I think the most I ever saw you bother with was lipstick."

A grin stretched across my cheeks. "That's the most I've ever bothered with. What's your schedule today?" I asked, shifting gears. "Cade sometimes works on weekends. I'm assuming you do too."

"Sometimes, but not today. The crews rotate weekend duty."

"Okay, so what are we gonna do today?"

My question elicited another slow grin from him and butterflies spun wildly in my belly. "Let's go into Anchorage. I need to pick up some gear for the crew, and I've got some errands to do. Plus, we haven't had dinner at Susitna Burgers & Brew in forever. It'll be like old times."

A giddy, bubbly joy rose inside. When you were in high school, the most exciting thing to do was go to the closest big city nearby. Given how rural Willow Brook was in the big scheme of things, it's proximity to Anchorage made the city seem amazing. At least, when we were younger. Having lived in Anchorage for a while when I was in college and then another large city out of state, the glow of city life had faded. But the idea of spending the day with Caleb doing something mundane in Anchorage and then stopping to have dinner at one of our old favorite restaurants was irresistible.

What followed was one of the best days I could remember in years. In fact, it might've been as long as since before the accident. It was odd that I didn't think of my small roll in the ditch a few weeks ago as much of an accident. The first accident was a dividing line in my life – the before and the after. There was always the weight inside my heart from it, the ache of losing a friend. I had carried on and became strong again in so many ways. But, just when I started to get my feet under me inside and think about making my own decisions again—decisions for me, not because I was simply running from the emotional pain— well, that was when everything started with Lance.

He'd ruined so many things for me. But this day, nothing particularly special about it, meant so much. He couldn't touch it.

Later that night, after running errands, including a solid hour spent in the gear shop for the fire station, we walked hand in hand into Susitna Burgers & Brew. Glancing around, it looked just as it had the last time I'd been here. It was a casual place with an open dining area with tables scattered in the center of the room and booths against the back wall. A bar was on one side and an open kitchen on the other. Exposed, weathered beams and polished wooden furnishings gave it a warm and cozy feel even though the space was large.

Slipping into the booth across from Caleb, I looked to him. My heart gave an odd skip and clenched, a feeling only he could elicit.

"Why don't you have some wine?" he asked when our waitress stopped by the table.

I shook my head. Seeing as he was driving, I figured we'd both stick to water. What followed felt like a hazy dream. Our dinner was relaxed and easy going. Aside from all the memories slamming into me, I was more relaxed than I'd been in years. If only because I didn't have that lingering anxiety I might be being watched. Even when I was just having dinner with friends in Portland for the last year or so, I never knew when I would later see photographs of myself sent over email or text.

It was late enough when we left that Caleb suggested we get a hotel because snow had started to fall softly while we'd been having dinner. Though it was only October, it wasn't out of the norm to have a bit of snow here and there. It wouldn't stay, but it was a harbinger of the winter to come. I didn't care to argue the point. At all. There was that, and the fact that I simply didn't want the night to end.

It didn't. I'd given up trying to come up with excuses to my parents why I wasn't coming home and just told them the blunt truth. I fell asleep with Caleb holding me close, boneless after another earth shattering climax.

I woke in the darkness, startled out of my sleep. The vibration of the phone woke me, the insistent sound of one text after another coming in.

The contrast of my internal state was jarring. I'd been in a deep sleep, more relaxed and peaceful than I'd felt in years. The novelty of being with Caleb was starting to wear off. It was feeling more and more comfortable.

Yet, I was highly attuned to that repetitive sound. There was only one person who ever texted me in the middle of the night like that.

I hadn't bothered to change the settings on Caleb's phone, so when his texts came in, there was a chirp. Yet, mine was set to vibrate. I couldn't help it, I had to see. I slipped out of Caleb's arms and tiptoed over to the dresser where I could hear the phone buzzing against the surface.

Caleb's voice startled me. "Ella?"

I spun around in the darkness. "Come back to bed," he said. He slid up on the pillows, beckoning with his hand.

I stared at him. The room was dim with hazy light filtering through the curtains from the parking lot. "I just want to see..." I started to say.

He climbed out of bed, moving swiftly. In a few quick strides, he was at my side, reaching past me to the dresser and snagging the phone off of it. Without even looking at the screen, he turned the phone off.

"Hey," I protested. "I wanted to see who that was."

He set the phone back on the dresser, his hands sliding from my shoulders down my arms. His touch was warm and reassuring. "You know who it is, and you don't need to worry.

That was the whole point of you not even worrying about your phone anymore," he said softly, his voice gruff with sleep.

"Yeah but..." *But I don't know how to let go.* The thought passed through my mind, colliding with another. This worry was what I'd considered my penance for the accident. Years later, it had stepped in to fill a role that I'd hated, but thought I deserved. Letting go of it was the only option, and I had to find my way through to that release.

I was tense, anxiety vibrating through me and dread churning in my gut.

"Ella, it's three in the morning. What's the point?"

"Why don't we just turn your number off altogether? I'll get a new number in my name, and you can just let that number die."

I knew it didn't make a lick of sense, but that felt like giving in and allowing Lance to win.

I looked up into Caleb's eyes in the darkness and sighed, letting my head fall against his chest. I hated it, absolutely hated how this whole situation made me feel. But I knew he was right, at least for now.

"I'll think about the number," I mumbled.

"And come back to bed?" he asked, his hand sifting through my hair.

I nodded against his chest. With a gentle tug on my hand, I followed him back to bed, falling asleep surprisingly quickly.

Chapter Twenty-One

CALEB

A week had passed since our night in Anchorage. In the intervening time, we had fallen into a rhythm. Ella insisted she couldn't stay with me every night. So about every other night, she would be at my house and at her parents' place in between. Meanwhile, she was actively looking for her own place to stay, which rankled me.

I knew what I wanted—for her to stay with me. Yet, I knew she needed to come to that conclusion on her own without pressure from me.

In the meantime, sporadic bursts of texts from Lance, or the asshole as I called him, continued to come in every few days. I had to give it to the guy, what he lacked in creativity, he tried to make up for with persistence. Rex had let me know the emails also came in similar bursts.

My patience with Lance's bullshit harassment was wearing thin. I'd vented to Rex about it the other day. He was just as frustrated as me, but he thought he had some movement with the help of his buddy in Anchorage. It galled me to no end that he kept repeating it would be easier to pin something on Lance if he had physically harmed Ella.

As if stalking her via text and email for over a year wasn't enough.

Cade kept tabs on the situation as well. Yet again, Ella encountered us once talking in her father's office. Her annoyance had been obvious. Her eyes had narrowed, and she chewed the corner of her lips, a sure sign of her frustration.

With those thoughts in mind, I drove home, hoping to see her that evening. We didn't plan ahead much. It was more happenstance that she would text and see what I was doing. I would invariably invite her over. Her parents had invited me over for dinner as well. That was nothing unusual, and nothing I hadn't done even while Ella wasn't living here. Cade was a friend, and Rex had become one in ways now that I'd been working on one of the crews at the station for a while.

That night, I arrived home to find my refrigerator empty and no text from Ella. I considered texting her, but decided to wait. I was hanging back more than I would like, if only because I saw how annoyed she got with any sort of pressure. I didn't know how much longer I could hang back like this, but I was trying to play it slow.

Creamsicle leapt down from the windowsill and onto the counter. I snagged a bottle of beer from the fridge, and he rubbed his cheek on the serrated edge of the cap where I set it on the counter. I stroked his back while he purred up a storm.

After a few minutes, restless, I strode to the windows and scanned the view. Autumn was a brief season in Alaska— a burst of color and then rapidly shortening days with winter nipping at his heels. Winter would be making itself known soon.

After another drag on my beer, I decided to go outside and chop some wood, needing something to do to burn off my restless energy. Within minutes, I was absorbed in the task, the force of the axe cleaving into the wood easing the tension bundled inside.

This thing with Ella was so unexpected and so intense, it was throwing me off. I wanted everything, all at once. More than anything, I want to erase her uncertainty, her tendency to hold back and her insistence on keeping me at bay in some ways.

With every thwack of the axe into the wood, I reminded myself it was worth the wait. As impatient as I might've been, there were years between us and more than enough baggage. Not to mention everything she'd been facing on her own.

As I chopped away, letting myself get into the rhythmic activity, Creamsicle meandered over and stationed himself on a stump nearby. He did that often—following me about the yard and observing whatever I happened to be doing from a safe distance.

After a solid hour of chopping wood, when I was good and tired, I returned to the house, feeling more settled inside. Creamsicle followed me back inside, bounding across the yard and dashing in through the door immediately. After a quick visit to his water bowl, he returned to his favorite perch in the windowsill.

A series of insistent buzzes on the counter caught my attention as I came out of the shower. I'd forgotten to bring my phone outside with me. I hoped it was Ella. But it wasn't.

It was another series of texts from the asshole, including two pictures of Ella and me when we had dinner last week in Anchorage. Hot fury raced through me, and then went cold. I was so fucking relieved she didn't have this phone. I did not want her see this. As much as it infuriated me, it scared the hell out of me.

Not for myself, but for her. Because it meant Lance was around and he wanted to push the envelope. For the first time tonight, I was relieved she wasn't here. Because I knew if she were here, I wouldn't be able to hide my tension. I didn't want her to know about this. Not until we had a plan.

Rather than texting Rex, I called him. He picked up on the second ring. "Hey Caleb. You don't call often, so cut to the chase," he said by way of greeting.

He was right about that. Though Rex and Ella's mother were good friends with my parents, and he had become a friend of sorts since I'd been stationed at Willow Brook Fire & Rescue, social chatting was something I saved for group situations.

"I wanted to call and give you a warning before I sent you these. I gotta tell ya, the only reason I'm not replying is because you told me it would be best if I didn't. I'm ready to hunt this guy down. But he's around and he has been since last week."

"What?" Rex asked, his tone low and cool.

Pulling my phone away from my ear, I quickly forwarded him the texts. "The pictures are going to show up in a sec. Ella and I had dinner there last week," I explained.

I heard a distinct chime through the line, indicating the arrival of my texts.

"Oh, this is bullshit," he muttered. "Ella's here, and I don't want you to talk to her about this."

"Trust me, I don't want to talk to her about this. We only have one problem. We know where she's staying. It's either there or with me," I said, abandoning any effort to ignore that detail. "But she goes to Anchorage once a week now. Somehow, we need to tell her he's around."

Rex was quiet for a beat. "Fuck."

Rex wasn't one to swear much, not as much as I did that was for sure. He saved choice words for moments when he was really pissed off.

"Well, you're right about that, but she doesn't go to Anchorage for another few days. I'm going to talk to Cade and see if we can come up with a reason for him to need that truck again. One of us can give her a ride. I'll do it or you can do it, but we'll figure it out. If I need to be at the station and Cade's crew is on duty..."

I cut in. "I'll talk to Ward. I'm sure he'll let me take the day off if I need to."

I knew we needed to figure something out, but I didn't feel comfortable lying like this. But I also didn't want Ella to get stressed knowing Lance was around. The only upside to all of this was if we could track him down, we could finally do something about him.

"Ella will be furious if she finds out we're doing this behind her back, but I don't want her to worry."

"Damn straight. I'm gonna call Cade right now," Rex replied.

I didn't like keeping this from Ella, but even more so I was furious Lance came all the way to Alaska. It turned my gut to think he was this obsessed with her. Within minutes, Rex called me back. He and Cade concocted a story where Amelia's truck was going to be broken down, so she would need to borrow Ella's for a few days.

According to Rex, Amelia wasn't thrilled about the plan and was only agreeing as long as we told Ella by the end of the week. After I finished my call with Rex, I called Cade.

"Hey man, I'm not so sure this is a good plan? Ella's gonna be pissed."

Cade's sigh was heavy. "Amelia's already cranky about it. She doesn't want to keep it from Ella and insists we have to tell her even if she gets stressed. But my dad is livid. He's worried that if we say something, Ella's gonna fight us on it, and she's damn stubborn."

I heard Amelia's voice in the background. Cade chuckled. "She's reminding me we get three days and that's it."

"Look, I'll just tell Ella I'm going to go to Anchorage for the day anyway. It's easier."

"That's probably better," Cade replied.

"I ordered some stuff for the station at the gear shop the other day. It's due in at the end of the week anyway. Ward was supposed to pick it up, but I know he'll let me do it if I explain why."

"Oh yeah. Forgot about that. I'll mention it to Ward tomorrow morning. He'll be doing us both a solid."

After I got off the phone with Cade, I called Rex back and explained the update. He agreed, thinking it was an easier fix.

Then, I called Ella. I felt silly knowing that she'd been in the house the entire time I'd been calling back and forth with Rex, but he'd explained she was busy grading papers in her room.

"Hey, what's up?" she said when she answered.

"I was just wondering the same of you," I replied.

"Grading papers. I meant to text you earlier and tell you I'd be working tonight, but I got busy."

"I figured. Thought I'd call anyway, I have to go back to Anchorage on Friday. I thought maybe we could ride in together. Isn't that the day that you have to go in for work?"

"Yeah," she said, pausing. I heard the sound of papers rustling. "You sure you don't mind? I'll be there from nine until three."

"If I minded, I wouldn't be offering. I need to pick up the order at the gear shop, and my mom needs me to pick a few things up at the hardware store." That was true, except for the fact that there was absolutely no rush. But I'd take whatever excuse I could. "If you want, we can just stay the night again," I added.

"Let's stay at your place. I feel bad leaving Creamsicle there alone."

I chuckled, glancing over at Creamsicle. I knew he was perfectly fine when I wasn't here, but he seemed to like Ella, so now she had a soft spot for him. "Whatever you want. I'm on a training rotation tomorrow, so I'll be tied up most of the day. How about I just pick you up Friday morning?"

"Perfect."

I hesitated as I held the phone against my ear, the words

I wanted to say caught in my throat. It wasn't as if I hadn't told her many times that I loved her. But that had been in our first iteration—ten years ago. I wasn't sure if she was ready to hear it right now. So I swallowed the words and said good night.

Chapter Twenty-Two

ELLA

Standing on the porch at my parents' house, a smile bloomed from the inside out when I saw Caleb's truck. It was early Friday morning. The sun was just coming up, its rays cast across the frosted landscape. As the frost melted, it misted the sky in a hazy pink and lavender with the sunrise in the distance. I breathed deeply, savoring the earthy scents of autumn.

We were leaving earlier than we originally planned. Caleb had texted yesterday and suggested we plan to have breakfast at one of our favorite diners. So with the crisp fall air and the scent of wood smoke in the distance, I jogged down the porch steps to meet him halfway.

I didn't even bother to keep myself from doing what I wanted. Catching his hand in mine, I reeled him close, leaned up and kissed him. He met me easily, dipping down and sliding his hand in my hair. His tongue swiped deeply before he drew back with a grin.

"You know both of your parents are watching us out the kitchen window," he said.

Flushing straight through, I rolled my eyes. "It's not like they don't know we're seeing each other. Anyway, let's go then."

Throwing my backpack over my shoulder, I walked ahead of him to his truck. The drive to Anchorage was gorgeous with the sun rising above the mountains and the mist slowly dissipating. As we drove and I absorbed the familiar views, I was feeling more and more like I was home, where I belonged.

Caleb dropped me off at the university, and I settled into a busy day. For the first time in too long, I was finally getting to do the work I wanted. That wasn't to say that my last job hadn't offered the chance. In fact, I'd thought it was my dream job on the faculty at the same university where I got my doctorate. I'd been hired on as associate faculty there. Yet, my enjoyment in burying myself in research had been short lived. Within six months, the texts and emails had started and I'd grown to dread going to work.

Here, my colleagues were friendly, everyone was busy, and it was all work. I spent the morning with another colleague who taught distance classes like me. We went over the curriculum together and then got up to speed on one of the projects where they were monitoring the tundra changes.

I loved digging into data. Some people found it boring, but not me. The day flew by. We also held a class with students who were there for a series of weekend classes. It was nice to actually meet some of the students I interacted with for online courses. Late that afternoon, Caleb arrived to pick me up, stopping in to greet a few of my new colleagues before we wandered off.

He glanced to me once we were in his truck. "I meant to find time to swing by the grocery warehouse today, but I was busier than I thought. Mind taking a run over there with me now?"

I grinned. "Of course not. I wondered why you didn't

pick up some groceries there last weekend. I've noticed your refrigerator is, um, kinda bare."

Unabashed, he simply shrugged. "I don't do much cooking for myself."

"How about you leave that to me?"

He chuckled and started driving, while I realized my comment held more weight than I considered. I'd slipped right back into this dynamic with him—where we felt *together*.

A short drive later, we were wheeling through the massive grocery store. I insisted Caleb stock up on some more dry goods and then he let me completely take over. I contemplated asking him to buy a chest freezer, hesitating when I realized I might be overstepping my bounds. I was getting *very* comfortable. In fact, I was starting to think like I used to think back when we were in high school before the accident. I'd been head over heels in love with him and convinced we'd be together forever. I had just enough maturity at that time—barely—to realize I might've been getting ahead of myself.

In the intervening years, with the emotional upheaval and then life getting in the way, I had largely convinced myself that my memories of my time with him were colored by our youth and I couldn't really have loved him that much.

But the way it felt to be with Caleb, well, it was like with no other man. Ever. There was that lingering pinch of guilt, but even that had faded enough I thought maybe, just maybe, I might finally learn how to let it go.

We were standing in line at the registers with Caleb's hand in my back pocket when he took a call from his mother. He paused moving the phone away from his mouth. "Mom needs me to grab a few things. I'll be right back. Don't get out of line though. You mind waiting?"

It was packed here. Every register was open and the lines stretched well beyond the waiting area in the front. I shook my head, waving him off. He turned and jogged away, still talking on the phone with his mother.

I shook my head with a laugh as I turned to face forward. Leaning my elbows on the cart, I waited as the line inched forward slowly. I'd been waiting maybe a minute or two since Caleb had left when I heard my name. A prickle ran up my spine, and the hairs on the back of my neck rose.

I knew that voice, but I had to be wrong. *It's nothing. You're in Alaska. He's not here.*

I carefully looked around, trying not to be obvious. But then I heard my name again. My stomach tightened and that heavy ball of anxiety I'd come to know so well settled in as if it had never been gone.

This time when I looked around, I saw him. I was so stunned to see Lance there that for a moment I froze. He was standing by the vitamin section near the pharmacy. There he stood with his dark blonde hair, always slightly mussed. Tall and lanky, he stared at me from across the store.

I forced myself to stay calm, but the panic was building inside. I wanted to turn and run through the store to find Caleb. But I didn't want to show my fear, not with Lance watching me. I knew that was what he thrived on— making me afraid.

I felt Caleb's presence approach from behind me. In the maybe three minutes he'd been gone, everything had shifted. He tossed a few things in the cart, glancing over to me. The moment he saw my face, he froze, his hand sliding down my back.

At the feel of his touch, I wanted to collapse into his arms. But I couldn't do that. Not now.

"Ella, what is it?" he asked, his eyes searching my face.

I swallowed through the fear caught in my throat. "He's here."

Caleb's eyes narrowed, but he didn't look away. "Are you talking about who I think you're talking about?"

I nodded, my motions jerky. "It's Lance. I don't want you to look. He's over there by the vitamins."

Caleb held still for a beat, his eyes assessing. "Ella, I'm gonna go talk to him, okay? You're not alone, and you're not going to be alone. Before I do, I'm going to call your dad. I just need you to act like nothing's happening. Just stay in line and check out. Can you do that?"

Staring at him, I felt myself nodding. Because it was the only thing to do.

Caleb didn't leave my side as he called my father. I listened to his half of the conversation. "Rex, Caleb here. Lance is here in Anchorage. We're at the grocery store." There was a pause as he listened to whatever my father said. "Yeah, she's okay. She's right here with me. I'm going to go talk to him and keep him here while she checks out. We have way too many witnesses for him to do anything stupid here. As it is, she's going to be waiting in line a good fifteen minutes before we get out of here."

I couldn't hear my dad's voice, just the murmur, and then Caleb handed me the phone. He waited while I spoke to my father. "You okay?" my dad asked.

I felt sick and cold. My hands were freezing, and I just wanted to run. I'd become inured to the anxiety while I had to face it every day, but I'd had a respite from it and now it was slamming back into me. But I knew it wouldn't help to say anything about that to my father. So I lied, but not completely. Because I would be okay. Caleb was here with me. "I'm fine, Dad. I mean, I'm not fine, but I'll be fine."

"Hang in there," he said simply. "You stay in line and let Caleb go talk to him. We need something to keep him there, and Caleb oughta tie him up for a few. We were worried this might happen after he sent those photos, so I've already updated the team there. I need to go so I can talk with them, okay?"

I must've said goodbye, but I didn't recall. With my phone clutched tightly in my hand, I waited, the time ticking slowly by. The murmur of voices around me faded to nothing but static.

All I could think was this was the reminder I'd needed. Just when I'd thought I could relax and find something good again, life reminded me why I couldn't.

Chapter Twenty-Three

CALEB

Tension coiled in every muscle as I came to a stop in front of the man who I knew to be Lance Wallace, if only because his gaze never left Ella the entire time I approached him. Crossing the warehouse, I had no awareness of our audience. My sole focus was the scum of the earth man standing there.

This man who got off on keeping Ella on edge, on scaring her, on trying to make her think he had some kind of hold on her. Cold fury was knotted in my chest. Stopping in front of him, I looked him up and down. He was the kind a guy most people couldn't stand. He gave off an arrogant, shady vibe. He was thin and wiry, his eyes a flat brown.

Knowing he worked in academics, I sensed he thought he was above most people. Perhaps he was in intellect, but he was a fucking asshole, the kind of asshole who used his career as a cover.

I didn't say a word. I just stared, standing close enough to force him to look at me. He was a coward. When he finally brought his eyes to me, I spoke.

"Leave Ella alone."

His lips curled in a sneer. "Haven't done anything to her. Who the fuck do you think you are?"

"That doesn't really matter. I know about your record. This isn't your first rodeo trying to bully a woman into giving a shit about you."

Lance barely even looked at me. His gaze honed in on Ella again. Glancing over my shoulder, I saw she was still in line. I needed to buy a few more minutes here. Just enough for the cops to arrive. I had no fucking clue what they planned to do as far as charges went.

"Don't even step a foot in her direction, you hear me?" I asked

Lance flicked his eyes to me, annoyance there. "It doesn't matter. Ella isn't meant to be with an idiot like you. I looked you up. I know you're her ex from high school and you saved her life in a car accident. You think that's why she cares? That's nothing. She needs someone like me, not some tough guy firefighter."

My anger went from cold fury to red hot. Not because this asshole insulted me. Whatever. It was the way he spoke about Ella, as if he had some kind of right to her. Spinning that into what I knew he'd been putting her through—just enough to make her feel crazy, just enough to make her feel nervous everywhere she went, every time she left the house —I wasn't thinking clearly.

I drew my arm back, intending frankly to drive my fist into the center of his sneering face. But then I heard Ella's voice and felt her hand on my arm.

"Caleb," she said, her tone low, quiet and controlled.

If anybody could've stopped me right that second, she was the only one. "Don't make a scene," she said.

Lance stared at her, a bitter laugh escaping. "See, she doesn't like the whole tough guy act."

Turning back to face him, I stepped closer. "You fucker," I bit out.

Ella's hand tightened on my arm, and she tugged. I didn't

know what the fuck she was doing, and honestly, I didn't understand.

"Ella, let me take care of this."

When she tugged on me again, the murmurs around us started to puncture the fuzz in my brain, my anger clearing just enough for me to remember we had quite an audience here at the store. At that moment, I heard feet moving quickly in our direction, footsteps striking against the concrete. Inside of a few seconds, two police officers were beside us with another hot on their heels. They glanced between us, one of them pausing to look to Ella.

"Ma'am? Ella Masters, I presume," the officer said.

At Ella's nod, the officer glanced from me to Lance, his gaze calculating. The other officer looked to me, nodding his chin to the wall nearby, indicating I should step back. I did not want to fucking step back. But Ella had her hand on my arm and was pulling me away.

We stood there and watched as the officers spoke to Lance. I couldn't hear them, but next thing I knew, they were sliding cuffs on his wrists. His gaze barely changed. He walked away, looking over his shoulder, his eyes on Ella the whole time. The man was fucking crazy, and it made me sick. Ella stayed quiet beside me, but I could feel the tension emanating from her.

One of the officers approached us. "He's being booked on charges of Second Degree Harassment. The DA will give you a call tomorrow," he said, directing his attention between Ella and me.

"How much do you know about how long this has been going on?" I asked. I wanted to make sure this wasn't going to be a catch and release situation.

"You must be Caleb Fox," the officer said, offering his hand. "I'm Officer Turner."

I shook his hand quickly and then arched a brow, expecting him to answer my question. He obliged. "Rex Masters has been keeping us up to date. One of our detectives has already lined up the charges if the guy ever came up here. Gotta say, we didn't actually expect that to happen. So this was a lucky break." He paused and looked to Ella. "Any questions ma'am?"

Her eyes bounced between us. "Not right now. I'd like to talk to the DA later," she finally said. She looked agitated and weary.

Something felt off, but I didn't have time to figure that out here in the middle of a busy grocery store with a police officer standing in front of us. "Can I get your number?" I asked before he turned away.

"Of course." He recited it quickly and also handed us each a card with his name and contact information.

I looked to Ella who had crossed her arms, wrapping them tightly around her waist. She didn't even look at me. She turned and walked quickly back to where our grocery cart was waiting unattended. It appeared she had asked the woman behind us to keep an eye on it.

"Thank you," Ella was saying as I caught up with her.

The woman beside her, with bright eyes and a smile, glanced between us curiously. All she said was, "Of course. Is everything okay?"

Ella nodded tightly and curled her hands over the cart handle, pushing it forward slightly. I stepped into line beside her, glancing down only to see her eyes trained straight ahead. It was more than obvious that she was trying not to look at me.

"Ella?" I rested an elbow on the cart to lean closer to her. "Are you okay?"

Her eyes flicked to me and then away, dark and guarded. I expected her to be upset, even angry at Lance's appearance here. "I just told you. I'm fine. I don't want to talk about any of this in here," she replied.

Uncertain what was going through her mind, I had enough sense to know now wasn't a great time to try to talk about anything. So I straightened and waited at her side as we got through checking out. Curious glances were cast our way, not exactly a surprise.

I resisted the urge to call Rex for a status update. I didn't want to make the call right now with Ella so clearly angry with me.

I slid my palm down her spine because I couldn't help but touch her, feeling the tension thrumming through her. For a beat, I felt her relax slightly before tensing again.

We checked out and then we were walking out to my truck. She stayed quiet the whole way out. When we reached my trunk, she silently handed things over as I put them in the back under the cab. I was closing it when she turned away and walked swiftly to return the cart. She climbed in without a word when she returned.

I didn't know what the hell was up with her, but it was stressing me out. Once I closed my door and we were in the privacy of my truck, I glanced over to her and turned sideways in my seat. "What's going on Ella?"

She crossed her arms again, staring forward with her fingers rubbing the edge of her jacket, an old nervous habit of hers. My heart twisted sharply.

"You knew he might be here," she finally said. "Why didn't you say something?"

I silently swore. This was exactly what I'd been worried about.

She finally turned to face me, weary pain contained in her gaze. "You could've just told me. You guys didn't have to come up with some ridiculous excuse for why you needed to be with me in Anchorage today. I would've wanted to come with you."

"Ella..." I started to reach for one of her hands, and she shifted back on the seat, shaking her head.

I ran a hand through my hair with a ragged sigh. "Look, I get it. I didn't want you to worry. He's already put you through so much. We were worried you were going to insist on coming by yourself. I didn't like it, but..." I paused, gathering my thoughts. Much as I could have considered shifting some of the blame for keeping this from her onto her father, I didn't want to. I hadn't wanted her to worry. "I'm sorry," I finally said because there wasn't much else to say.

She swallowed, the sound audible in the small space. She finally nodded and looked forward again. "Let's just go."

"Ella..." I started to stay, but she wouldn't look at me. Something else was simmering under the surface with her, but I didn't know what it was.

We drove home in silence. When I pulled up at her parents' place, she practically leapt out of my truck. Before closing the door, she looked to me. "I think we should take a break."

Pain bolted through me, and a flash of anger and old hurt rose inside. "You shut me out once before, but if that's what you're going to do again, there's not a fucking thing I can do to stop you."

I heard her breath hiss sharply, but right now I didn't give a damn.

Chapter Twenty-Four

CALEB

Another few days passed, during which Lance's harassment of Ella seemed as if it might finally come to an end. Between everything Rex had compiled with Ella giving him permission to delve into her past history of emails and texts, Lance was being charged with multiple crimes. All in all, it was rather anti-climactic. At least for me, that is. When all was said and done, he was facing charges here in Alaska and Oregon. His attorney was arguing he should be extradited down there, which was perfectly fine with me.

The further away from Ella he was, geographically speaking, the better. Yet, my anger and frustration at the effect it had on Ella were hard to vanquish with the slow, methodical legal process. Meanwhile, Ella and I were barely speaking.

If I were being honest with myself, I had to admit I was frustrated with her too. I'd thought myself long over the pain caused when she broke up with me after the accident. Yet, the way she pushed me away in this process hit too close to home. Because that was exactly what she had done before.

I loved her. Yet, it burned to have her keep me at arms

length like this. Again. For her to think that letting someone who cared about you try to be there for you was taking over, well, it just sucked.

Closing my locker at the station, I shook my thoughts away. Just as I turned to leave the locker room, Cade walked in. He paused by the door. "Everything okay with you and Ella?" he asked, not even bothering to say hello, but then Cade had never been one to waste time.

When I shrugged, he eyed me for a long moment and then shook his head. "Ella can be stubborn, but then so can you."

"What the hell do you mean by that?"

Cade hooked a hand in his pocket, narrowing his eyes. "Look, I get it. Things happen, but don't let your pride get in the way. I did that and I'd give anything for those seven years back with Amelia."

I stared at him for a long moment, trying to shake the tension building inside. "Yeah, well, it's not that simple. Plus, Ella was the one who broke up with me back then and now. Not the other way around."

Cade rolled his eyes. "I know you're a few years younger than me, but I guess you missed the news back then. Amelia broke up with me too. She had her reasons. As I did for staying away, but I could've fought for her a helluva a lot sooner. If Ella means as much as you said, then fight for her."

He didn't give me a chance to respond and simply spun on his heel and walked away. That pissed me off. "Thanks for nothing," I called after him.

He stopped at the doorway, turning around and lasering me with his gaze, his green eyes so similar to Ella's. "She loves you, you know. Figure it out."

This time he left for good, and I kept my mouth shut.

At that moment, Ward Taylor, the superintendent for my crew, came around the corner into the lockers. His eyes flicked in the direction of Cade's retreating back and returned to me. It was obvious he had heard most of what had just been said, at least the last exchange.

I liked Ward and respected him, but I sure as hell didn't want to get into a conversation about my relationship, or lack thereof, with him. I managed a tight smile and turned to close my locker. I was relieved when I heard the sound of his locker opening and then closing. I turned to leave, thinking the moment had passed.

No such luck. Ward was standing there, leaning against the lockers, his eyes waiting for me. Ward was tough as nails and a damn good superintendent. He tended to be quiet and could be intimidating until you got to know him. His soft spot was his wife, Susannah. All she had to do was walk into a room, and he practically turned to mush. Lately, unless we were out in the field actively dealing with the fire, he tended to be on edge and worrying about whether she was going into labor. She was due any day now and had gone past her due date.

This meant a cranky Ward, but we were all putting up with it because his worry was so obvious. He was a man who liked to control what was happening and it was driving him near crazy he couldn't in this case.

His gray gaze caught mine and he arched a brow. "Need some relationship advice?"

I bit back a sigh and then shrugged. "Not really."

"It's none of my business, but I'll say this. If she means something, don't let her walk away."

———

The next day, Ward was off because Susannah finally went into labor. Meanwhile, as the lead foreman on the crew, I was in charge when we got called out to a large fire out at a hunting lodge. Alaska had hunting lodges and cabins scattered everywhere, so this was nothing unusual. This particular lodge served as a fairly high-end hunting and fishing resort.

Though it was approaching winter, the lodge still had guests. The lodge was within a fifteen-minute flight of Willow Brook but completely off the road system, so we geared up and headed out. Thoughts of Ella fled in the heat of the fire. Our crew and Levi's responded.

As we flew overhead, we could see the fire from the sky. The lodge was surrounded by nothing but forest and wilderness including a few sections of tumbledown spruce still holding strong in the bark beetle kill ravaged forest. Considering that we were heading into winter, I wasn't as worried as I might've been if it were spring or summer. We were due for some rain in the next few days. If we could manage to get this fire under control and get the guests in the lodge out to safety, we'd call it a win. Fred Banks, the pilot who helicoptered us out gave a wave and said he'd return when we radioed.

My brother Nate had radioed while we were en route to share he'd be flying out soon with a water delivery. Nate, like many bush pilots in Alaska, was licensed to fly planes and helicopters and often helped our crews with air water delivery during fires. Though this particular fire wasn't that remote, as remote goes in Alaska, they had no local water source beyond a well and a river nearby.

I conferred with Levi once we were on the ground. We quickly developed a game plan and then spread out. First order of business was to get the guests out of the lodge. The lodge had a central wing and two side wings. Guests were trapped upstairs in both of the side wings.

Levi's crew handled one wing, while mine took care of the other. Despite being in the wilderness, this was luxury lodging with large suites, dining areas and more. It was also set up for people to stay for long chunks of time. This lodge was open all year with hunters, fishermen, hikers and the like coming during spring, summer and fall, while backcountry skiers came during the winter.

A few of the guests and the owners had acted quickly and done what they could to isolate the fire where it started in the kitchens. Yet, with three stories and an almost full lodge, not everyone had gotten out. With the flames shooting high in the sky and burning up the log structure, we needed to act fast. I glanced to Jesse, who shared foreman duties with me. "I'll head up. How about you guys get the ladders out?"

Jesse nodded. We were in an unusual situation here. Often in backcountry fires, we'd be limited with our equipment. But the lodge had stored ladders high enough to reach the windows in an outbuilding, so we had options.

I glanced over to the crew. "Thad, Donovan, you guys up to coming with me?" I asked. Both nodded. I knew the answer without asking, but out of habit, I asked.

Jesse and the rest of the crew hustled over to deal with the ladders. Tugging on my breathing apparatus with Thad and Donovan following, we made our way into the downstairs. Smoke was thick. We could hear the rushing sound of the fire from the center of the structure. A factor on our side, but also a mark against us, was that the structure was log. The logs gave the fire fuel, but they would burn more slowly than lighter weight building materials. Yet, if it got too hot, we'd be in trouble.

We headed up the stairs. According to the owner, there were two groups of guests on the third floor. Glancing at the windows once we made it to the third floor, I could already see the ladders. I didn't even need to tell Thad and Donovan what to do. They immediately started checking the rooms up here. After we fanned out, I came across an elderly couple who were both struggling with smoke inhalation. I wasn't confident they could handle a ladder rescue.

Thad and Donovan worked quickly, separating out who was deemed safe to take down the ladders and who would need to be carried down. They got going with helping guests out the windows and down the two ladders. Meanwhile, I had to do something I hated—make a choice over who needed to get out faster. Both the man and woman in the couple were frail and coughing heavily. Honestly, I didn't know what the hell they were doing out at a remote lodge in Alaska.

When I glanced between them, the man caught my eyes. "Please take her first. If I need to, I can handle the ladder," he said in between coughs. I handed him my respirator to give him a few fresh breaths and then put it back in place.

With another glance to Thad and Donovan, I counted out seven others who still needed to be helped down. No time to wait. I lifted the woman into my arms and carried her out swiftly. She was small, frail, and easy to hold. The smoke was getting thicker, and I could hear the fire quickening in the center of the structure. I distantly wondered how things were going over on the other end of the lodge, but I stayed focused, moving quickly down the stairs and outside.

After handing her over to the medical team, I immediately ran back inside. It was blazing hot, the heat penetrating my heavy gear, and I knew I didn't have much more time. Reaching the top floor again, I saw Thad and Donovan were helping the last two guests out the window. Relieved, I approached the man who was waiting where I'd left him. I gave him a few more breaths of oxygen before fitting the respirator back on. He insisted he wanted to walk, but I shook my head no. I could move quicker with him in my arms.

We made it out within minutes with Thad and Donovan right behind us. After delivering the man to our medical team, I met Levi just outside the center of the structure. Their timing had been about the same as ours. According to the owners, everyone was accounted for now. A brown dog was scampering about the yard. He paused by Levi and me, licking my hand as I slipped my gloves off.

"We need water to help with this fire," I muttered once I tugged my respirator off.

Levi nodded. "Should be any minute now," he said.

As if on cue, we heard the distinct sound of helicopter blades coming from the distance. I wondered if it was Nate. Obviously, there was no way for me to know from here, but I'd be able to check on the radio shortly. Meanwhile, Levi and I got back to work, heading out to create fire breaks in the area surrounding the lodge to hopefully contain the fire to the structure alone. Darkness wasn't far off, so we needed to get this done as quickly as possible.

Late that evening, I sat on the ground, leaning against a tree and guzzling a bottle of water. Rolling my head to the side, I glanced at Levi. "Don't suppose we'll get an update if Susannah had the baby yet."

Levi flashed a tired grin and shrugged. His face was covered in sweat and grime just like mine. It had been a long afternoon and evening. The fire was under control, but the structure was still smoking. Between our crews and the guests at the lodge, we had way too many people to ferry out of here. As it was, it looked like quite a few of us would be spending the night here, so I planned to volunteer. For the first time in hours, Ella danced along the edges of my thoughts.

As if he read my mind, Levi commented, "I'm going to have to radio Lucy. I figure I'll volunteer to stay for the night. You in with me?" he asked.

"I was just thinking the same thing. It's almost dark. Let's check with Jesse and see if he's heard back from Fred and Nate. I don't even know if they can do another run tonight."

Levi nodded, cupping hands around his mouth. "Jesse!"

Jesse Franklin turned from where he stood with a few of the other guys. Strolling over, he stopped in front of us. "What's up?"

"Have you heard on the radio if they can make another run tonight?" I asked

"That's a no. They just radioed in and said it's too dark. That was my guess anyway. We got our gear, so we're good for the night. The water is actually still working out in that building," he said, gesturing to a small outbuilding.

"You're fucking kidding me," Levi said.

Jesse chuckled. "Nah man. It's a cleaning area after guests come back from hunts. No hot water, but I'll take what I can get."

We settled in for the night with the guys. I fell asleep later, tired and with Ella drifting through my thoughts, spinning on repeat in my brain. I missed her. So damn much.

Chapter Twenty-Five

ELLA

Almost a week had passed. In the interim, Lance had been arrested and charged. According to my father, he'd be extradited to Oregon soon. In the meantime, I hadn't spoken to Caleb or much of anyone beyond my parents. One evening, Amelia all but badgered me into going to girls' night, this time hosted by Lucy at the home she shared with Levi. With the others enthusiastic approval, Holly was coming along with me. In fact, she was my ride. I wasn't in much of a mood, but I knew if I kept avoiding everyone, there would be too many questions.

Seeing Lance in Anchorage had set me back and reminded me why I just couldn't expect things to work out with Caleb. That was asking too much from the universe. Even though it seemed like maybe, just maybe, Lance would finally be held accountable, it didn't change the emotional playing field for me. Seeing him had been a jolting reminder of why I couldn't expect to settle into something good with Caleb. Hoping for it was too much.

I tried to keep up a good front and managed to glide by

everyone's radar so far. With the birth of Susannah's baby earlier today, everyone was mostly focused on that. We were ensconced at the kitchen table when I saw a brown and white hamster scurry across the floor. Glancing to Lucy, I arched a brow. "Do you normally have a loose hamster running around the house?"

She smiled and nodded. "Oh yes. That's Levi's hamster, creatively named Ham. He's been here longer than me. He pretty much does whatever he wants, and Levi feeds him by hand. It's rather adorable really."

I tried to imagine Levi feeding a hamster by hand. The picture was rather incongruous — Levi with his rugged firefighter vibe and this tiny brown and white hamster. Lucy scooped Ham from the floor and handed him over to me. Ham glanced up at me, his little brown eyes wide. I stroked my fingers down his back and watched as he meandered about the table, sniffing the cards.

Maisie was running late, so we played a hand before she arrived. Amelia, Lucy, and Maisie had respectively stopped by the hospital to visit Susannah earlier. She was spending one night there and then would be heading home tomorrow.

With all the chatter about the baby, I didn't find out until we were into our second hand that Caleb and his crew had flown out to a fire with Levi's crew. I was busy trying not to let that bit of news bother me. Considering I was with three women who were married to hotshot firefighters, it didn't feel right to fall apart over it in front of them. Yet, my heart squeezed, and guilt stabbed at me. I'd broken up with him. Again. My worry for him pierced through the numbness I'd pulled around me like a blanket.

Maisie's arrival distracted me. She watched while Lucy triumphantly won yet another round. Lucy glanced over to Maisie. "See," she announced gleefully.

Maisie arched a brow. "See what? I already know you can win when I'm not playing."

Amelia chuckled. "Yeah, we all know that Lucy."

Lucy sighed elaborately and then shuffled the cards, motioning for Maisie to join us at the table. Holly glanced around the table. "I can see this is serious," she observed.

I nudged her with my elbow, still forcibly keeping my worry off of Caleb. "You're telling me. They don't mess around."

Lucy dealt the cards. "It's just something fun for us to do. Plus, you two are fresh meat."

Holly didn't miss a beat. "I'm not fresh anything. I've been in Willow Brook forever, I know everyone's secrets," she said with a sly grin.

"So true," I offered with a small smile. "Any news on the baby?" I asked, looking to Maisie.

"He's adorable of course. Susannah lost a lot of blood, that's why they're keeping her for the night," Maisie replied.

"Is she going to be okay?" Holly and I asked in unison.

"Yeah, I'm not exactly sure what happened. Ward was a mess about it in the waiting area. He settled down after they let him go back to see her. The nurse came to tell us she was fine, so I figured it was a good time for me to leave."

Lucy looked to Holly. "You're a nurse, what causes something like that?"

Holly cocked her head to the side. "I'd rather not guess. If they said she'll be okay, she will. I'm sure she's tired as hell no matter what."

Amelia nudged Lucy with her elbow. "She'll be fine, and you're up."

Lucy studied her cards before laying two on the table. Maisie glanced over at Amelia. "You're next."

"Next for what?" Amelia countered.

"Having a baby," Maisie said with a wink.

Amelia sighed. "I still can't decide."

Maisie rolled her eyes. "Well, don't wait too long. This second pregnancy is making me exhausted," she said as she rubbed her belly. "I figured it would be easier because I've done it once, but no such luck."

Lucy's phone buzzed and she laid a few cards on the table before glancing at the screen. The teasing expression faded from her face quickly, and she answered. "Hey what's up?"

She nodded along, her eyes flicking over to me. "Uh huh, uh huh. Okay. I love you." She tapped to end the call and looked over at me. "Caleb and Levi will be spending the night out there with some of the other guys." Her eyes landed on Maisie next. "I'm surprised you didn't already have the update."

Maisie shrugged. "I'm not on duty. You just got the update. They've been shuttling people back and forth all afternoon. How many are left out there for the night?" she asked.

I tried not to look too focused on Lucy, but my heart was tightening. My worry went up another notch inside.

Lucy shuffled her cards, seeming rather *not* worried. "Levi didn't say. He said it's too dark for the rest of them to fly out. On the upside, there's running water in one of the outbuildings where they clean the fish and stuff."

"Stuff?" Maisie asked.

"Well, it's a hunting and fishing lodge, so I guess stuff would be carcasses," Lucy replied matter-of-factly as she eyed her cards.

Maisie rolled her eyes. "Good grief, you didn't have to say it like that."

"Well, what else should I call dead animals?" Lucy countered.

Holly giggled. Only in Alaska would we be talking about dead animals and fish over cards.

"Is everyone okay?" I asked, unable to hold back any longer, my gut churning.

Lucy's eyes landed on mine. For a moment, I thought she was going to tease, but she appeared to reconsider. "Of course. Everyone's fine. We would've heard sooner if they weren't. Have you heard from Caleb?"

I silently groaned as too many pairs of curious eyes swung my way. I hadn't really talked to anyone about the fact that I'd told Caleb we needed to take a break. Just now though, I was questioning everything. The oh-so-familiar guilt of feeling as if I didn't deserve to have a shot at happiness was clashing with my sudden guilt at boxing Caleb out. Again.

The only person here who knew anything was Amelia. She'd tried to talk to me about it the other day, and I'd brushed her off. I had plenty on my mind and simply hadn't been up to dealing with a pep talk. Dealing with the police here and in Oregon in the aftermath of Lance's arrest had kept me mentally occupied.

I was beyond relieved about that, but it had been an emotionally exhausting few days. I'd had to go through everything with them. Again. Meanwhile, unless Lance pleaded out, they were warning me to be prepared to testify. I might need to fly to Oregon for it. I would cross that bridge when I came to it, or at least that was what I kept telling myself every time I thought about it.

Amelia's eyes flicked to mine. Much as I wished she would keep her mouth shut, she appeared to decide otherwise. "You haven't, have you?" she asked pointedly.

I took a gulp of my wine and flicked my eyes her way, biting back a retort. On a sigh, I answered, "No, I haven't."

Holly glanced sideways, her eyes narrowing. "Why not?"

Oh well, oh hell. I'd have to suck it up and be honest. "I, uh, told him we needed to take a break."

Holly sighed elaborately. "You've got to be fucking kidding me."

Emotion knotted in my throat. I swallowed, willing myself to get a grip.

"You *need* to move on. Don't let the past get in the way. Again," Holly said bluntly.

Amelia piped up. "Okay, I don't know what she's talking about, but Caleb obviously loves you. Cade says he's been a mess the last couple of days. You look miserable too, so what gives?"

I didn't know how to explain myself. If only because, all of a sudden this kernel of worry about Caleb made it all seem so ridiculous.

Lucy appeared to let go of her reconsideration to stay out of it, her eyes catching mine. "Seriously, that guy adores you."

I fiddled with the cards in my hand, glancing to Lucy and chewing the corner of my bottom lip. "It's not that simple," I finally said. "I know Caleb..."

My words ran out. Because what I'd been about to say was that I knew Caleb loved me. I didn't doubt it. Not for a second. I thought back to the first time I broke up with Caleb. I'd been picking my way through the rubble of my shock from the accident and the confusion I'd created for myself by pushing Caleb away at a time when I needed him so much.

After those weeks when I'd been discharged from the hospital, I'd been at my parents' house with my mother hovering. Meanwhile, I was still in recovery. I limped around with crutches for a while due to the injuries on my leg. I grew to dread the looks cast my way from peers—a hint of confusion and pity with a giant dollop of thank-fucking-God-that's-not-me.

Holly had been dealing with her own grief, her worries about me, and everything was all tangled up together. We managed to keep our friendship cobbled together, but it was challenging. When I was all better and got the chance to spread my wings and fly away from home, I did so with a vengeance, clinging to the hope that I could escape the grief and guilt that had caught me in its web.

I'd thought I could inoculate myself from the pain and

accept that I could never make up for Jake's death. All of these thoughts were spinning through my mind as I glanced around the table. Yet, I found four equally stubborn, independent and strong women staring back at me. After the long silence, Holly broke it. "You know, you're stubborn as hell. Don't let your guilt get in your way with Caleb again."

"I'm not being stubborn. Not this time," I muttered, defensiveness rising sharply inside.

Holly held my gaze—her eyes fierce. "You are."

I almost burst into tears, but I held it together. The tightness bundled around my heart eased slightly, and I couldn't say why. After a beat, Holly looked away and laid a card down on the table, nudging me with her elbow. "You're up."

Her comment signified the end of everyone airing their opinions of Caleb and me, which was a relief. I managed to relax, if only because they let the topic drop and conversation moved on. Maisie called into the hospital to check on Susannah and the baby. With a good report, we all toasted to her and then finished our game.

As Holly was driving me back to my parents' place, we approached the road that led to Caleb's house. I suddenly wondered if I should check on Creamsicle. I glanced to her. "Hey?"

Eyes on the road, she slowed. "What?"

"I'm gonna call Caleb and see if he wants me to check on his cat."

A smile curled the corner of Holly's lips. "Oh really?"

She knew where Caleb lived. Willow Brook was tiny, and most everyone local knew where everyone else lived. She turned onto his road, commenting, "Go right ahead and call him."

Pulling my phone out, or rather his phone, I tapped to call him. I wasn't sure if he'd actually answer or if he even had reception, but seeing as Levi had been able to reach

Lucy, I was hoping for the best. He picked up on the second ring.

"Hey," he said, his voice more gruff than usual.

My heart knocked against my ribs. "Are you okay?" I asked. "I heard from Lucy you'd be out there for the night, but your voice doesn't sound good."

"Just a long day and a lot of smoke here earlier," he replied.

My heart squeezed and I suddenly got anxious, thinking it might be silly to ask if he needed me to check on his cat. But I was already on the phone, so I forged ahead. "I thought I'd see if you wanted me to check on Creamsicle."

He didn't reply at first, so I kept talking. "I mean, if it's okay. I could even stay there and keep him company."

Caleb was quiet for another beat and then his soft laugh filtered through the line. "I'm sure he'd love that, and of course you can stay. I should be home tomorrow, probably midday based on the weather report."

"Okay." I paused, emotion thickening my words. "Do you have somewhere warm to sleep?"

"You worrying about me?" he countered.

I could hear the smile in his voice.

"Maybe. Holly's dropping me off at your place."

"Good to know. If you need my truck, the keys are in the drawer by the door."

"Your truck is there?"

"Yep. I caught a ride with Donovan earlier. He lives right down the road from me."

There was more I wanted to say, but we had a curious audience in Holly, so I kept it simple. "Good night. Call me in the morning, okay?"

"Good night." There was a long pause, while I gripped the phone tightly in my hand. "Miss you Ella."

I almost burst into tears. "Miss you too," I replied, the words simply slipping out.

I tapped the screen to end the call and took a deep

breath. "Don't say anything," I ordered, glancing sideways at Holly.

"Uh, okay." With a shake of her head, Holly rolled to a stop in front of Caleb's house. "Want me to stay with you? We could have a girls' night."

Angling sideways in the seat, I grinned. "It's fine with me, but let me call Caleb back. I mean, it's his house."

Holly chuckled while I quickly called Caleb. His tone sounded puzzled when he answered. "Yeah?"

"Can Holly stay with me?"

"Not that you needed to ask, but of course," he replied with a little laugh. "Is that it?"

"Uh huh. Call me in the morning when you think you'll be on your way back."

My cheeks were hot as I ended the call. "Okay, slumber party," I announced, a giddy joy bubbling up inside. We were adults and far past our childhood when we used to have slumber parties all the time, but it was yet another thing that made me feel like I was really home.

Holly followed me into Caleb's place, glancing around as we entered. "Wow, this place is nice," she commented. "I remember when he was getting it built because Nate was jabbering to Alex about all the solar stuff he was getting done."

"Here, I'll give you a tour," I said, gesturing for her to follow me.

I was a little tipsy from the wine, and I felt flushed inside and out from my brief call with Caleb. A sudden wave of longing hit me as I started walking up the spiral staircase. I'd missed him the last few nights. I sighed internally. Holly was right. I could be stubborn.

After I showed Holly through the upstairs and we returned downstairs, there was a meow from the front deck. As soon as I opened the kitchen door, Creamsicle dashed through. He twined around my ankles before scampering over to his water bowl and food. Meanwhile, I looked through the cabinets to see if there was any leftover wine or beer.

Holly and I settled in to watch television. We finished off a bottle of wine and spoiled Creamsicle as he settled himself between us on the couch and purred up a storm.

Chapter Twenty-Six

ELLA

The following morning while Holly and I were enjoying coffee, my phone rang. I answered immediately when I saw it was Caleb.

"Hey, do you know what time you'll be back? I was thinking I could plan to pick you up."

Instead of Caleb's voice, Levi Phillips' voice greeted me. "Hey Ella, it's Levi. Small delay."

"Is Caleb okay?" I asked quickly, my heart beating rapidly as anxiety coursed through me.

"Oh, he's fine except he broke his leg," Levi replied nonchalantly. "I was assigned to call you and let you know."

Panic knotted in my chest.

"Why are you so calm about this? What happened? Are you sure he's okay?" My questions flew out, one after the other, barely a pause between any of them.

Levi chuckled. "I'm calm because there's nothing to freak out about. I'm not happy he broke his leg but he's fine. I swear. Here."

There was a rustling sound, the sound of footsteps, and then another rustling sound before Caleb's voice came through the line. "I promise I'm fine," he said, his tone slightly pained.

"What happened?"

His frustration filtered through the line with his sigh. "Something stupid. The fire was pretty much out, and we were checking the building. A beam fell on my leg. I should've waited a little longer, but it is what it is. As soon as the helicopter gets here, they'll take me straight to the hospital when I get to the station. I'm trying to convince Levi the hospital isn't necessary, but he's being a pain in the ass about it so far."

Intellectually, I knew this wasn't a major thing. He had a broken leg, nothing more. But panic spun through me, clanging loud and metallic in my thoughts.

I didn't realize I was crying until I sniffled slightly. Caleb's voice softened. "Look, it's okay. It's a fucking pain in the ass, but I'm fine. Not a big deal."

I hiccupped. Holly had stepped into the bathroom when the phone rang and came out at that moment, her concerned gaze sweeping over me. I pulled the phone away from my mouth to explain. "A beam fell on Caleb, and he broke his leg."

Her eyes widened and then she shifted into her practical mode. "Well, I've gotta go because my shift starts soon. Tell him I'll see him at the hospital later. I'll call you as soon as he gets there."

Caleb must've heard what she said because he replied. "Tell her she can count on it."

"I'll meet you there," I said quickly. "Any idea when they'll fly you out?"

"Not yet. The fog is thick this morning. Once it clears, we'll be on our way."

I heard several voices in the background and Caleb replying to them before speaking to me again. "Babe, I gotta go."

"Okay, I'll meet you when you get here."

I held onto the phone until the line went dead in my ear. Then, I set it on the counter and promptly burst into tears. Holly was sliding her jacket on and walked back over to the counter beside me, resting her elbows on it.

"You okay?" she asked.

I dragged my sleeve across my face and sniffled, nodding as I did. "I don't know why I'm crying. I mean, he's fine. It's just his leg. Right?"

Holly rubbed my back, her eyes softening. "Yes, lots of people break their leg every day. I'm sure he'll be fine once it's set. But maybe you should think about why you're falling apart over this."

I mustered a glare and another hiccup to go along with it. "Fine. I'll see you later at work. Because I'm coming to the hospital as soon as he gets there. Promise you'll call me?"

Holly grinned. "Of course. You need a ride?"

"No, Caleb said last night I could use his truck."

Holly arched a brow, but said nothing as she spun away. "See you later," she called as she walked through the door.

A few hours later, I hurried into the hospital, not even bothering to check in at the reception desk. Inconveniently, I was stopped as I started to hurry down the hallway.

"Excuse me ma'am."

Glancing over my shoulder, I saw a young man in scrubs. "Yes?" I asked, trying and completely failing to rein in the impatience in my tone.

"You need to check in at the desk before you go back there," he explained.

Feeling rushed and frantic inside, I bit back a curse. It wasn't his fault he was getting in my way. "I'm here to see Caleb Fox. He knows I'm coming."

The man wasn't swayed. "You still need to sign in."

Oh well, oh hell. With a huff, I spun around and hurried

back to the reception desk. After quickly reciting my name and signing in, I was given permission to go.

Once I reached the room where Holly told me Caleb was, I didn't even think to knock and just shoved through the door. Dr. Lane, or Charlie to me, was standing beside an examining table talking to Caleb. She glanced back, her gaze concerned. "Excuse... Oh, hi Ella, what are you doing here?"

Why didn't everybody know I had every right to be here instead of asking me all these questions? With another sigh, I opened my mouth to explain, but Caleb beat me to it.

"She's here to see me, Doc," he explained. "If it's okay with you, can she stay?"

His eyes were on mine, and butterflies spun wildly in my belly. Only Caleb could give me that look while he was waiting for his broken leg to be set and looked to be in a bit of pain.

Charlie glanced between us and then shrugged. "It's up to you of course. I'm not up on all the gossip around town. Are you two together?"

"Yes." Pushing past all the uncertainty inside and closing the door behind me, I walked to the examining table, rounding to the opposite side from Charlie. "How are you?" I asked, curling my hands on a bar on the side of the table.

Caleb had one leg resting on the table and the other hanging half off the side. His hair was mussed, and his eyes were weary. He smelled faintly of smoke, and I wanted to cry again. I swallowed against the emotion thickening in my throat and tried to breathe slowly.

"I'm fine. Doc here is going to get this casted up and then I'll be good to go," he explained, gesturing to his right calf. "I won't be driving though, not for a while." He reached for one of my hands, his grip strong and warm. "Don't look so worried. It's not a big deal."

Charlie chuckled and glanced between us. "You firefighters. Doesn't seem to matter what happens, you bounce right back. This one is going to take a bit though. Don't you dare let him drive until I clear it," she said, her eyes flicking to me.

I nodded, rather emphatically. "Of course not."

She lifted a clipboard resting on the counter behind her. "I'll be back shortly."

When the door clicked shut behind her, the room got quiet. I simply stared at Caleb, absorbing the sight of him—the clean, strong lines of his face, and his dark chocolate eyes. He was leaning back against the pillows. He looked tired, but relaxed. Tears still pressed hot against my eyelids—not from sadness, but from a mingled sense of joy, confusion and regret.

Why in the world a simple thing like his broken leg would nudge me past the logjam inside of my heart and mind, I didn't know. I loved him. The fear and anxiety I'd been carrying inside for the last year or so had shut me down again. The mess with Lance and how it all played out had worn on me.

When you're young and a friend dies, you eventually learn that it scars your heart, but the scars heal and you carry on. The scars don't go away, but they do change you. All that time we'd been apart had made me forget so much. I couldn't change the past, but I could change our future.

Caleb's hand was still curled over mine, and he gave it a gentle squeeze. "You okay?" he asked.

I didn't realize I was crying until I felt the cool trail of a tear on my cheek with more tears wicking up from the knot of emotion in my heart. "What is it with hospitals? I seem to cry whenever I'm near one," I muttered with a swipe of my thumb across my cheek.

For some reason that made me laugh. It started as a regular laugh and then it just kept going. By the time I caught my breath, Caleb was grinning, simply watching and waiting. "Are you done with that now?" he asked when I finally managed a few breaths without laughing.

With a hiccup, I nodded, snagging a tissue from the

counter behind me, yet not daring to let go of his hand. "Uh huh."

"What's so funny anyway?"

I sobered quickly, lifting a finger to smooth over his brows. "I don't know. I love you."

He held my gaze for a long, searching moment before tugging me to him quickly. Sliding his arm around my waist, he rose up to pull me close. "I love you too. But I suspect you already knew that."

I barely managed to nod before his lips were on mine.

The sound of the door opening snapped us apart. Charlie entered with a nurse and a med tech. Her eyes bounced between Caleb and me, a smile playing at her lips. She didn't say a word. Seeing as we had an audience and they had a job to do, I stepped out of the way.

Chapter Twenty-Seven

CALEB

Three weeks later, I glanced at my phone where it sat on the coffee table by the couch. Leaning over, I snagged it. Dammit. A pillow slipped to the floor in my effort to reach the phone. Creamsicle looked over from his perch on the windowsill. Aside from the minor injuries I'd sustained in that car accident years back and some other minor injuries during the last few years as a firefighter, I'd never had any injury where I was laid up the way I was this time. I'd sustained a fracture in my right tibia, which was a pain in the fucking ass. According to Dr. Lane, it would be six to eight weeks before I'd be cleared to return to regular duty for work.

I couldn't drive either. In short, I was mostly laid up on the couch with the exception of Ella or my family carting me around wherever I needed to go. It was fucking annoying. Today, Ella was in Anchorage, so I was home alone with Creamsicle for company. He was none too impressed with my lack of activity.

Getting my damn cast off couldn't come soon enough if you asked me. Ward had offered to set me up with light duty, but that was filing and a bunch of bullshit I didn't want to deal with. I'd asked if I could just take the time off. Ward was in a damn fog over his new baby, so he'd simply nodded and signed off on it.

After I retrieved the errant pillow from the floor, I pulled up my text screen and tapped out a message to Ella.

Hey, when will you be back?

As soon as I finished typing, I stared at the screen, waiting for her reply. After a moment, I tossed the phone on the couch with a groan. I had never in my life stared at my phone and waited for someone to text me back. But I was bored out of my mind.

Just as I was about to force myself to get up and take a shower, my phone buzzed. Lifting it, I saw a return text from Ella.

Bored? :-)

I grinned as I tapped out my reply.

Bored out of my fucking mind. I think next time you go to Anchorage I should come with you.

You'll be sitting around all day! I'm working and you can't drive.

I glared at my phone screen. She was completely right. Obviously. But I would've given a lot for another night at Susitna Burgers & Brew with her. A night where I could be guaranteed Lance wouldn't ruin our evening by sending photos later.

He was in Oregon out on bail, but under strict orders and with a monitoring bracelet. Apparently, he'd been stalking another woman from his old job all along. When they started doing some digging, they'd quickly discovered that trail. He was in enough trouble that he would be staying put.

I tapped out another text.

Maybe you could pick up some takeout on the way back. Grab something from that Thai place we love, and we can heat it up here. Please.

Of course. Text me what you want, and I'll get it on the way back. I'm leaving in an hour.

Miss you.

Have to go. I've got a class to teach. <3

With another sigh, I levered myself up, grabbed my crutches from where they were leaning against the side of the couch and hobbled into the bathroom. I missed sleeping in my bed. The spiral staircase—which had seemed brilliant when I had the house built—was a pain in the ass for crutches. Thank God the sectional couch actually had a pull out bed for sleeping. But it wasn't my bed, and I was tired of being trapped downstairs.

I needed to shower before Ella got home, and two hours gave me plenty of time for that. By the time she got our food and drove home, I'd be ready. I was bound and determined to snap her resistance to sex. She'd somehow convinced herself I was made of spun glass, and we shouldn't have sex while I had a cast on. Fuck that. I missed her. I missed her naked, and I missed being buried inside of her.

As promised, Ella arrived roughly two hours later. The time in between our small texting conversation and her arrival had actually been productive. I'd taken a shower, I'd done the stretches that Dr. Lane recommended to keep from getting stiff, and I'd even washed Creamsicle's water bowl and given him fresh food.

He still didn't seem too impressed by me, but then he was damn hard to impress. Ella came walking in the kitchen door, her arms laden with bags of books, her laptop carrier, groceries and the Thai food I had requested.

I was conveniently sitting on a stool by the counter, nursing a beer and flipping through some magazines my brother had dropped off. My instinct was to ask her if she needed some help because I surmised she had more groceries than what she brought in. But helping with my leg would make more work for her than it would be if I just stayed put.

Damn. I hated being helpless like this. Because my mouth couldn't listen to the instructions from my brain, I called over, "You need any help?"

As soon as I spoke, my mouth caught up with my brain. "Ah hell. I won't be much help."

Ella paused by the couch, setting down her laptop and her books before walking over to me by the counter. After setting the bags of groceries on the counter, along with the takeout, she turned to face me. A smile tugged at the corners of her mouth, but I could tell she was holding it back. She lost the battle when a soft laugh escaped.

"What's so funny?"

"You are terrible at this."

With a shrug, I reached for her free hand, tugging her to me. She stepped carefully between the cage of my cast and my other leg, which was propped at an angle on the rung of the stool.

I brushed a loose lock of hair away from her eyes and tugged her a little closer, savoring the hitch of her breath when she bumped against my torso. Damn. I didn't think I'd ever get enough Ella. Just now, seeing her here with her long brown hair in a tousle around her shoulders, her mossy green eyes darkening with desire, and the feel of her lush breasts against my chest—heaven.

"I am," I murmured, pulling her closer and fitting my mouth over hers.

I meant for it to be a quick kiss, but it was as if a flame whipped to life around us. In a flash, her tongue was tangling with mine, my heart was thudding against my ribs, and lust was lashing at me.

Ella broke away, much sooner than I wanted. Her lips were swollen and her pupils dark and wide with her breath coming in little pants. I could feel the tight points of her nipples pressing into my chest. I took full advantage, sliding my hand down her spine to cup her sweet ass, letting my fingers tease just along the crease between her thighs.

"Caleb, you have to stop," she murmured.

"Why? All I did was break my leg. I'm fine."

"I have to get the rest of the groceries," she murmured, her cheeks pinkening as I stared at her.

"Okay, go get the groceries."

I reluctantly let her go, not because I wanted to, but because I could be strategic when necessary. I waited at the counter, taking a few more sips of my beer before she returned with the rest of the groceries. I got up and hobbled around on one crutch, opening the cabinets and helping her put things away as she handed them over. I sensed she wanted to protest even this small task, but I was prepared to remind her that Dr. Lane had said I needed to move around when I could.

I'd never have thought putting groceries away could be a turn on, but right now it was. With the sweet scent of Ella drifting up to me and a subtle buzz of need coursing through my veins, my body was running on high idle.

After we got the groceries put away, Ella swatted me back to the counter, and she transferred the Thai food to plates before heating it up quickly. While we ate, I watched as she twirled the chopsticks around the noodles, realizing just how bad I had it for her. As her lips parted and her tongue darted out to catch a loose noodle, blood shot straight to my groin.

I forced myself to focus on dinner and actually managed to eat. A fucking miracle given that I couldn't stop staring at Ella's mouth with every bite she took. Just when I thought it couldn't get worse, she ran her tongue along the chopsticks when she finished. Fuck me.

Ever focused on what she was doing, Ella got up to put everything in the dishwasher. She refused to let me help and ordered me to rest on the couch. I decided that was just fucking perfect when she leaned over to adjust the pillows behind me. She was wearing a blouse from work with the buttons stretched tight across her breasts. A hint of navy lace peeked out. Unfortunately, the temptation was brief when she returned to the kitchen.

Creamsicle was focused on something out in the field, his tail twitching back and forth as he sat on the windowsill. Calling over my shoulder, I said, "You might wanna let Creamsicle out."

Ella simply opened the kitchen door. The moment Creamsicle heard that, he dashed across the room and outside. Darkness was falling, and the air was crisp. A gust of wind blew inside with a hint of wood smoke. If I hadn't been burdened with a cast on my leg, I'd have gotten up to make a fire. I wasn't quite up for that, and I didn't want to ask Ella to take care of it. She returned to the couch with a beer for me and a glass of wine in her hand. With the couch doubling as a bed, she couldn't simply sit down. I shifted over to create more space beside me when she settled at the end towards my feet.

A grin curled her lips as she took a sip of wine and set it on the table behind the couch. Moving up beside me, she tucked her feet under her knees and eyed me. "What should we watch tonight?"

"You pick. I've watched just about everything these last few weeks. Find something I haven't seen yet and make me love it."

She giggled, and I caught her hand in mine, tugging her towards me. I moved quickly, not giving her a chance to think and pulled her right onto my lap. Conveniently, as if I'd actually planned it that way, her knees fell on either side of my hips. She giggled again, her eyes flicking to mine and her cheeks flushing.

"Caleb, what are you doing?"

"This."

I fit my mouth over hers, threading my hand into her

hair and pulling her tight against me. I didn't even bother to take it slow. My cock was hard the minute her hips settled over me. I slid my other hand down her spine, cupping her bottom and rocking my arousal into her. She gasped into my mouth, giving me the perfect opening to sweep my tongue into the warm sweetness of hers. Startled enough, she didn't resist, her hips sinking into mine and rocking against me.

I needed to taste her. With a groan, I tore my lips free of hers, dragging my tongue down along her neck, savoring the salty, sweet tang of her skin.

"Caleb," she murmured on a low moan as I nipped at her nipple through her blouse. She made a weak effort to protest. "We have to stop. You need to be careful with your leg."

I laved my tongue over the thin cotton of her blouse, tugging at the buttons. "This isn't bothering my leg at all, and it's not going to," I murmured, lifting my gaze to meet hers. "If you want to make me feel better, give me this."

Ella's gaze held mine, her eyes darkening. For good measure, I flexed my hips into hers, savoring her sharp gasp. Reaching between us, I flicked the buttons loose on her blouse. She didn't stop me, although I could see the hesitation warring with desire in her eyes.

"Caleb," she muttered again.

I traced a nipple with my fingertip, squeezing it lightly and watching as her teeth sank into her plump bottom lip. "Yes Ella?"

"You're supposed to rest," she protested. Her body betrayed her with a roll of her hips over the hard ridge of my cock.

"I've been resting for three weeks. Trust me, this won't keep me from resting. In fact, I'll sleep much better."

A giggle escaped, her cheeks flushing a deeper shade of pink. "But..."

I decided to take matters into my own hands, or rather into my mouth. Much as I wanted to tease her breasts, I needed her to stop talking. Thumbing one nipple, I threaded my hand in her hair and fit my mouth over hers. With a sweet sigh, her tongue slid against mine and our kiss went wild. I fucking loved kissing her.

Her hands cupped my cheeks, and she dove into our kiss, her mouth as greedy as mine. Meanwhile, I flicked my thumb on the clasp between her breasts, groaning at the feel of her breasts tumbling loose. "Fuck Ella," I murmured against her lips when I drew back to gulp in air.

She leaned back, her lips puffy, her eyes wild, and her skin flushed. "You are nothing but trouble," she said, her voice husky and a hint of a smile teasing the corners of her mouth. "If you hurt your leg, I'm telling Charlie this is all your fault."

"Go right ahead," I said magnanimously, knowing that she wouldn't say a damn word because she'd be mortified. I also wasn't the least bit worried. I, on the other hand, didn't give a damn if Charlie knew I hurt my leg burying myself to the hilt inside of my sweet Ella.

Her cheeks flushed deeper, and she rolled her eyes. But then, she made me forget everything—everything but her. She stood, quickly shaking her blouse free from her shoulders, her bra sliding to the floor with it. With a shimmy of her hips, her leggings joined the pile of clothing.

My cock was so hard, it was a damn miracle I hadn't already come. Ella, being as solicitous as she was, stepped closer to me and adjusted the pillows around me. As she leaned over, I cupped one of her breasts in my hand, catching the nipple in my teeth. With a swirl of my tongue, I drew it in with a deep suck. She cried out and then drew back, her eyes flashing. Curling her hands over the waistband of my sweatpants, she tugged them down, teasing me by not even touching my cock, which was rock hard and ready. She carefully shifted my sweatpants down around my hips and then straddled me again.

Nothing but the thin silk of her panties was between me

and paradise. I looked up at her—with her hair falling around her shoulders, her nipples playing peekaboo through the dark locks, her skin flushed and her eyes flickering with desire. I reached up, brushing my thumb across her bottom lip and groaning when she caught it in her teeth and sucked it into her mouth. I rocked my hips into her, savoring the damp heat of her through the silk. Drawing my thumb free, I trailed my fingers down, tracing a nipple with the dampness before dipping down over her belly and then sliding my fingers over the thin silk of her panties.

I didn't bother to take this slow. I'd had enough of that already. Shoving the silk to the side, I sank my fingers into her slick core, watching as she arched back, her breath hissing. Her channel clenched around my fingers.

"Look at me," I said gruffly.

Her eyes opened slowly. I fucking loved the look of her when she was like this. It felt as if we were all alone in the world and surrounded by a shimmering curtain of desire. I didn't care to ever escape.

"I'd love to watch you come on my hand, but I don't think I can wait that long. More than that, I want you to come all over my cock."

Her lips parted and her eyes widened as I drew my fingers out. Adjusting the angle of my hips, I held still for a beat, the head of my cock nestled at her entrance, its slick heat calling me. She rose up, her eyes on mine, and sank down slowly, taking me in, inch by inch, until I was fully seated inside of her.

Chapter Twenty-Eight

ELLA

Caleb's dark gaze held mine. The room was quiet, save for the soft sounds of our breathing. My heartbeat, pounding fast and true, echoed through my body. His hands slid down my sides to curl around my hips. With a flex of his hips, his cock stretched my channel. The feeling was so delicious, it sent a hot shiver through me.

It had been three long weeks where I'd been holding back. But right here, right now, everything else fell away. Everything but the feel of him filling me. My eyes started to fall closed on the heels of another arch of his hips into mine.

"Look at me."

His gruff command drew my gaze to his again. I started to rock with him, rising up and sliding down, sheathing him in my core again and again. I felt pulled tight inside as pleasure spun within me.

I couldn't look away as he gripped my hips. My clit, slippery and wet, rubbed against him as we rocked together. Pleasure splintered through me, hot slivers of fire with every flex of his hips into me. This moment felt wild and out of control, spiraling madly. Yet, it also felt suspended in time—

in a haze of passion and intimacy that ran so deep, it struck me straight at the heart.

This wasn't just sex. The scars on my heart and those on my body were mementos of everything we'd walked through together. We'd walked through our own fire and come out to the other side where the flames of this new fire could rise from the ashes of the old.

He slid a hand free from one of my hips, stroking up my back in a heated pass and levering me closer. His lips caught mine in a slow, sensual kiss. He drew back as I rocked my hips into him, every spark of sensation feeding into the pleasure flashing through me.

His palm slid down over my belly, dipping into my curls and pressing on my clit. Everything inside drew together tightly and then unraveled in a burst of pleasure. My channel pulsed around his cock, clamping down tightly. I felt the heat of his release fill me when I collapsed against him, dipping my head into the curve of his neck as I struggled to catch my breath.

Pleasure pinged through my body in little aftershocks. Caleb's skin was damp, as was mine, but he was warm and he smelled so good. He smelled like him—a woodsy scent mingled with a crisp freshness that I loved.

One of his hands rested on my back and the other curled over the dip at my waist. Once again, I felt that strange sensation where his thumb stroked back and forth over the soft skin of my belly and then along the edge of the scarred skin on my side. I doubt he even noticed it. I did.

After a few moments, I managed to lift my head. Before I realized it, my question slipped out. "Do you even notice them?"

He adjusted his shoulders against the pillows and opened his eyes. "Notice what?"

There was my answer.

He arched a brow in question. "My scars."

His gaze flicked down, his thumb stilling where it was. "No," he finally said, his eyes rising to meet mine again.

I lifted a hand, tracing my thumb along his jaw. "Well, you got what you wanted."

He laughed softly and shrugged. "See, I'm completely fine. I bet I'll sleep better than I have in weeks tonight."

———

The following morning, it was Saturday, and I was in the kitchen starting coffee while Caleb showered. I'd woken up on the sofa bed with my head tucked into his shoulder. His arm was wrapped around me and held me close against him. In that hazy, dreamy time, I felt completely safe, as if I was exactly where I was supposed to be. Even with my old doubts, Caleb managed to make me feel as he always had. Just right.

Pulling out the eggs, I heard a thump and then a muttered swear. Setting the eggs on the counter, I hurried across the room and into the downstairs bathroom, pulling open the glass door to the shower. Caleb sat there, his hips resting on the corner seat in the shower.

"Are you okay?"

He glanced over to me, his eyes annoyed. "I'm fine. Just slipped."

"Do you need help?" I asked, stepping in the shower, not even paying attention to the damp floor until the moisture seeped through my socks.

He curled his hand into mine. I helped him to standing and got him out of the shower onto the less slippery surface of the dry tile floor.

"Have I mentioned I can't fucking wait to get this cast off?"

"You might've mentioned it," I said with a laugh, realizing he was perfectly fine. "When do you see Charlie again?"

"Not soon enough. It's been three weeks, and I get my first checkup next week. She warned me it would be six to eight weeks, but it feels like forever."

Stepping back and tossing my now wet socks in the hamper, I rested my hands on my hips and eyed him. "You keep saying you're fine." I bit my lip to keep from laughing.

"I'm fine, but this sucks," he muttered as he dried off.

I left him as he tugged a pair of sweatpants on, while I jogged upstairs to find a dry pair of socks. I returned to making omelets. After we finished eating, he asked me to drop him off at the station for the day. It was Saturday, so I cast a puzzled glance his way.

"Are you sure?"

"You're running errands, and for fuck's sake, I am so sick of hanging out at the house."

"Are you..." I bit back my question. For the third time this morning, I'd been about to ask him if he was okay.

A smile tugged at the corner of his lips. "I'm fine."

I stepped to where he sat on one of the stools by the kitchen counter. Without missing a beat, he tugged me between his legs. Shamelessly, he slid a hand down my spine and cupped my bottom. Need rolled through me in a flash.

"Oh no, you're not starting that now."

Lacing his free hand in my hair, he pulled me within an inch of his lips. "I might be a little cranky, but it's pretty awesome to have you fussing over me."

"Does that mean you're going to stop complaining about being laid up?"

A bubbly joy spun inside of me, mingling with a clench of my heart, so tight the emotion almost made me cry. He shook his head, murmuring *no* against my lips just before he kissed me. His kisses slayed me—every single time. Inside of a hot second, I felt as if I was caught in a flame. Then he was drawing away, his eyes catching mine.

"Don't forget I love you."

EPILOGUE

Caleb

Six months later

I stood at the top of the ski slope. It was winter, and the sun was high in the sky, bright against the blue backdrop. Lifting my eyes, I took in the view as I turned slowly in a circle. Mountain peaks rose behind me and to the sides. Kachemak Bay was visible in the distance, the sun striking sparks on the surface of the water.

Ella and I had come to Last Frontier Lodge for a mini-honeymoon. We'd gotten married two days before and intended to spend a few more days here. The ski lodge was roughly four hours south of Willow Brook in Diamond Creek, yet another stunning town in Alaska. Owen and Ivy Manning, who'd designed my house, had invited us down after the wedding.

Ella was waiting at the lodge, and I needed to ski down this mountain to get to her. With a push of my ski poles, I curled forward and flew down the slope, the snow spinning in an arc around me when I reached the bottom. With a wave to Cam Nash, Owen's brother-in-law and retired world-class skier who happened to make his home here, I headed into the lodge.

After a quick trip to our room to change out of my gear, I made my way to the restaurant. I found Ella typing away on her laptop. Since she'd moved in with me officially, I'd learned she did *not* know how to take a break from her work. Not that I was complaining. At all. I couldn't really, given that my job took me away for weeks at a time.

I walked up beside her in the booth and dipped my head, dropping a kiss on the side of her neck. Angling her head up, she smiled. "I was just finishing up," she murmured.

In the last six months, we had settled into a comfortable routine. She mostly worked from home, while I stayed busy dealing with whatever came up for my crew. Creamsicle kept her company anytime I needed to be gone. Though we'd yet to face the busiest time of year for me, spring through fall, I wasn't worried. I'd miss her like hell, but she'd be there when I came back.

I slipped into the booth across from her, taking in her tousled dark hair, her mossy green eyes and the way her teeth dented her bottom lip as she finished typing before she closed her laptop. My eyes flicked down to her hand where she wore a simple platinum wedding band. She hadn't wanted anything else. She wasn't much of a diamond girl, and that was just fine with me.

Lance was in jail. The charges related to Ella had held up, along with a few more connected to two other women. He had a pattern, and it was a damn miracle he'd managed to stay in respectable positions. He'd faced charges in California, Oregon, Washington, and Alaska. In the end, the charges from here and Oregon were enough to put him away. I was damn relieved we hadn't had to even think about him recently.

As I sat there, looking across the table at Ella, I couldn't quite believe she was here, and we were married. I'd never have guessed that her car rolling into a ditch seven months or so ago would've brought her skidding back into my life.

Delia Hamilton, the lodge restaurant's chef, paused by our table, her honey blonde hair catching the lights from the restaurant. "So how is everything?" she asked with a warm smile.

"Perfect," Ella replied, glancing up at her.

"Do you need something to drink?"

"I'll take some of your hot cider. You?" I asked, catching Ella's eyes.

A slow smile teased her lips, and she nodded. With a nod, Delia turned away. She ran the kitchen at the lodge and had been nothing but welcoming. Her hot cider had quite a kick, and it was sublime on cold winter days. We'd been here for the weekend, and I'd quickly become addicted to the stuff.

While we waited, I reached across the table to catch Ella's hands in mine. "Are you ready to go to Hawaii?"

She cocked her head to the side and nodded. "Absolutely. Although it's nice here. I'd heard they did a ton of renovations while I was in grad school. But... Wow. It's pretty crazy that this place used to be empty."

"I think it's been about five years since Gage came back and renovated it. Anytime you want to come down here again, let's do it. I love it here, plus it's good to see Owen and Ivy."

Delia delivered our cider, checked to see if we needed anything else and then spun away, leaving us alone. I glanced out the window at the snowcapped mountains and then back to Ella, realizing it didn't matter where we were. Not to me. Don't get me wrong, Hawaii would've been nice about now. It had been a long, cold winter. While the days were getting longer now, sometimes the darkness could wear on you when you only had five or six hours of sunlight during the dark months of winter.

Later that night, I walked to the windows, watching the

sunset over the mountains. Our room offered a view of the slopes and angled out toward Kachemak Bay. The sun slipped behind the mountains, its rays casting pinks and lavenders across the water as it ruffled under the breeze.

Ella's hands were resting on the windowsill. I stepped behind her, sliding my arms around her waist and dipping my head to breathe in her scent. Her hand slid up to cup my cheek as she angled back to catch my eyes.

"I still can't believe you're here," she murmured.

"Oh, I'm here," I said, catching her lips in a lingering kiss. "I'll always be here."

———

ELLA

A few weeks later, I rolled over, coming awake slowly to feel myself surrounded in Caleb's embrace. He was warm, but then he was always warm at night. I loved it.

We never made it to Hawaii. I couldn't believe it, but the following day, I had fallen going down a ski slope and badly sprained my ankle. Yet again, something had happened and intervened with our plans. But I didn't care. Not even a little bit. We stayed at the ski lodge for a few extra days and then came home.

My ankle was just about back to normal. I felt Caleb shift in his sleep, and I nestled my bottom back towards him, smiling when I felt his arousal against me. I kept thinking this ridiculous, out of control desire would start to fade now that we'd been together a while. If anything, the opposite appeared to be happening.

In the wispy light of dawn with desire curling around us like smoke, I rolled over when he said my name.

"Yes?"

"Good morning," he said softly, dipping his head and catching my lips in a kiss. As was always the case, there was no such thing as just a kiss with us. A good hour later after he'd left me boneless from a shattering orgasm, we showered and made our way downstairs. I leaned against the counter and sipped my coffee as Caleb got ready for work.

This—these mundane moments—were my favorite part of our life together. Small gifts like this were something I'd written out of the story for myself before my life intersected with Caleb's again. He stood, snagging his bag of gear and turning back as I followed him to the door.

"When will you be home?"

"Maybe I shouldn't even leave," he replied, his gaze darkening.

My cheeks heated. "No. You go. I have work to do, and you said you guys had some projects today."

He winked and swung his bag over his shoulder.

"I love you," I called as he opened the door.

He looked back once more. In a flash, he grabbed my hand and reeled me to him again. He claimed my lips fiercely, leaving my pulse pounding as he drew back. Walking backward, he blew me a kiss before turning. Closing the door behind him, I leaned against it and simply smiled.

———

Thank you for reading Burn So Good - I hope you loved Ella & Caleb's story!

Up next in the Into the Fire Series is Sweet Fire - Jesse & Charlie's story.

Keep reading for a sneak peek!

Be sure to sign up for my newsletter for the latest news, teasers & more! Click here to sign up: http:// jhcroixauthor.com/subscribe/

JESSE

I stared at Dr. Lane, fighting the urge to tell her to go to hell.

"Did you just tell me to go to hell?" she asked without even looking up from the screen on the small computer tablet she held.

So much for keeping my thoughts to myself. She finally looked up, pushing her glasses up on her nose as she did.

"I guess I did," I finally said with a sheepish smile. "I can't believe you're making me wait another two weeks before clearing me for full duty."

She cocked her head to the side from where she sat on a rolling stool by the counter. Her gray eyes scanned my face, and I wondered what the hell she was thinking. She was so fucking uptight.

I was at a doctor's appointment for a follow up after I dislocated my shoulder for the second time in a few months. Dr. Lane was a new doctor in Willow Brook. I was used to

Dr. Johnson, or Doc as I called him, a rather cantankerous older man who definitely wasn't as uptight.

Damn if she didn't get under my skin. With her dark hair always pulled back, and her glasses, she gave off a distant vibe. For god's sake, the woman wore her hair in a bun. I had no idea what her body looked like because she was always shrouded in a white lab coat. I suspected she had a banging body, or at least my cock thought so. Every damn time I saw her, I got tense — all over.

I rolled my offending shoulder, ignoring the slight twinge of soreness. "Helen said it was fine and I might be ready to be cleared," I explained, referring to my physical therapist.

Dr. Lane was not nearly as warm and friendly as Helen. My physical therapist had a grandmotherly warmth to her and made me feel better every time I saw her. Unlike Dr. Lane who made me feel tense and irritable. If only she would clear me to return to full duty, maybe I could relax.

Dr. Lane adjusted her glasses again, turning her head slightly as she set the computer tablet on the counter. As she turned, I noticed for the first time that she had a streak of purple in her hair. Damn. I did *not* know what to make of that.

Before I had much time to contemplate the implications of said purple streak, she spoke. "I could, but honestly this is the second time you've dislocated it in a couple of months. I think if you wait a little longer before you push it too far, you probably won't have the same problem again. I know you're frustrated with me, but I actually do have your best interests at heart."

I bit back another curse. Even if she made me tense, I wasn't an asshole and prone to telling women to go to hell. I took a deep breath and ran a hand through my hair as I let my breath out in a sigh. I might've been annoyed, but I wasn't an idiot. "Fine. I get your point. Helen said the same thing. She's just a little easier to persuade than you," I said, flashing a grin.

I couldn't say why, but that streak of purple relaxed me. I supposed it cued me to the fact Dr. Lane might not be as uptight as I'd assumed. Dr. Lane's lips twitched, but she didn't say anything. Something about her made me want to ruffle her feathers. Big time.

Except for days like today, the only other times I'd seen her had been on the heels of shift when I was dirty and grimy from dealing with a fire. Perhaps that was why she set me off—the contrast of her tidy form in comparison to mine. I was a hotshot firefighter, so when I came in after a day's work, I was about the opposite of tidy. It also annoyed me to no end to deal with injuries. I'd now landed in Dr. Lane's office twice due to dislocating my shoulder.

"So you don't mind waiting another two weeks?" she asked.

I shrugged, my shoulder giving a slight twinge as I did, which should've been my cue that waiting was smart. I was bored out of my fucking mind being off of duty. It wasn't that I couldn't work. There was plenty to do, but I was relegated to light duty tasks when I preferred myself to throw myself into work. I loved my job as a firefighter. I loved the hard work and the physical challenge.

"I'll manage it," I finally said, sliding my hips off the examination table and standing.

It just so happened that Dr. Lane stepped off of the rolling stool at precisely the same time. When I lifted my head, I found her standing barely more than an inch away from me. Remember how I said she made me tense?

Lust slammed through me at her nearness. She smelled good, a wisp of lavender drifting up to me. Her eyes flicked up to mine, widening slightly. This close, I noticed her gray eyes contained a hint of violet. Her mouth parted slightly when she gasped, drawing my eyes right to her lips. I'd never even noticed her lips before.

Just now, I became acutely aware that they were full and soft. Damn, I wanted to kiss her. She stepped back quickly, her hips bumping into the counter against the wall behind her. The clipboard she'd been holding clattered to the floor.

"Oh shit!" she blurted out as she leaned over to pick it up.

Unfortunately or fortunately, depending on how I looked at it, I leaned down reflexively at the same time. Our hands brushed and a jolt of electricity zinged through my arm. Her head bumped into my shoulder.

When she straightened, her cheeks were flushed pink. If I thought I'd wanted to kiss her a minute ago, now it was close to irresistible. I shackled the urge.

Meanwhile, the tidy Dr. Lane looked flustered and embarrassed. For the first time, I wasn't annoyed with her. She finally seemed human.

"So you swear," I said with a wink.

Her cheeks flushed a deeper shade of pink. "Obviously I swear," she finally said.

It was almost as if I could see her internally gather herself back together. She straightened, smoothed a hand over her hair, and then adjusted her glasses. I was starting to get the idea that might be a nervous habit of hers. I'd have given just about anything to see her hair loose.

My words were ahead of my brain. "Do I make you nervous?"

Slick dude. Because that'll help her relax.

I caught myself about to roll my eyes at my own thoughts.

Dr. Lane looked taken aback by my question. She adjusted her glasses again, looking down at the clipboard I held in my hands. I handed it over to her, and she clutched it tightly to her chest.

"I don't know if nervous is the right word," she finally said. "You seem annoyed whenever you're here, and I'm sorry for that."

Her answer took me off guard. "Oh." For a moment, I

almost denied that I'd been annoyed both times I'd been here. But what the hell? It was the truth. Until now that was.

I shrugged. "Sorry about that. It's not your fault I dislocated my shoulder twice. I don't like being injured."

She smiled—and promptly took my breath away.

Her face transformed, her eyes tilting at the corners and her warm smile softening her sharp features. "I don't suppose anyone likes being hurt. Plus, you have a demanding job, and I imagine it's hard for you to take a break."

"That's one way to put it," I answered wryly, shackling my body's out of control response to her. I needed to get out of this small room because her scent was filling my head and making me crazy. Just as I considered what to say to quickly leave, there was a knock at her door.

CHARLIE

I stared into Jesse Franklin's eyes, little charges of electricity tingling through me from where we'd collided. My cheeks were hot, and I was flustered. But then, every time I saw Jesse Franklin, I was flustered. His gaze held mine—a rich, clear green. I'd never seen a man with eyes like his. With his dark amber hair tousled and wavy, his fit body, and his rugged features—a strong jaw, a prominent nose and angular cheekbones—well, he was unnervingly handsome.

His eyelashes were so thick, they nearly curled to touch his cheeks. It didn't seem quite fair for man to have eyelashes like that. Nature had been generous to Jesse Franklin in the looks department. His mouth had a sensual look to it, always making me think completely inappropriate thoughts. He was a patient for god's sake. He'd only been to see me for his dislocated shoulder. But still.

I clutched the clipboard to my chest as if it could shield me from the heat dancing through my body. For the first time ever, he didn't seem annoyed with me. As I tried to gather my scattered thoughts into something sensible, there was a knock at the door. Thank God. My body had been frozen in place about an inch from Jesse whose physical presence was so potent, it made me a little crazy.

I stepped back, nearly dropping the clipboard again. Quickly opening the door, I found my medical assistant Rachel there. She smiled, glancing between Jesse and me. "Mrs. Stan is here to see you."

I stared at her, her warm blue gaze unable to calm the anxiety that suddenly swirled inside of me. *Mrs. Stan* was code for a personal issue that had become way too common in my life lately. Worry galloped through my thoughts. I started to hurry out the door, coming to an abrupt stop when Jesse said my name.

"Do I need to make another appointment?" he asked.

Flustered, I turned back to him, adjusting my glasses and trying not to sound too worried. "Of course you do. I'm sorry to rush off. Just a small emergency. Sandy in reception will schedule your next follow up. In the meantime, keep going to see Helen and I'm confident in two weeks, we'll be able to clear you for work."

Jesse held my gaze for a beat, and yet again heat bloomed through me. Under the circumstances, I couldn't believe my body's reaction to him. Because lately, my life had been anything but inviting for desire or romance. In fact, I'd put those ideas on ice.

As I started hurrying down the hallway, Jesse walked with me, easily keeping pace with his long stride. I was too frazzled to make polite conversation, turning into the door that led to my private office as soon as I reached it.

"I'll see you in a two weeks," I said quickly before stepping into my office and closing the door behind me. Leaning against it with a sigh, I took several slow breaths to calm my pulse. I couldn't relax though. I hurried over to my desk, snatching my cell phone off of it and hitting speed dial.

My mother picked up on the first ring. "Where are you?

Your father's not home yet, and this doesn't seem like home."

A bite of grief slammed into me. I took a slow breath and swallowed my tears. "Hey Mom, I'll be home in just a little bit, okay?"

"Where is your father?" she countered, her voice confused.

"He won't be here tonight," I finally said.

I listened as she asked me a few more questions, and I answered with my usual rote answers, trying to keep my tone level and the worry out of my voice. After I hung up, there was a quick knock at my door. "Come in," I called out.

Rachel stepped through the door, closing it behind her. "Everything okay with your mom?"

I looked up into her warm gaze. I wanted to burst into tears, but now definitely wasn't the time. "She's fine. I wish she would remember my dad's dead." My heart thumped another beat of grief.

Rachel's eyes searched my face, but I battened down the hatches inside and took a deep breath. I could handle this. Snagging my coffee mug off my desk, I took a sip of the long cold coffee, the cool bitterness fortifying me.

"Hey, at least Jesse Franklin wasn't too cranky with me today," I said with a chuckle.

Rachel grinned. "I noticed." She paused, cocking her head to the side with a gleam entering her gaze. "I think he likes you."

"Huh?" I asked as I shrugged into my jacket and snatched my purse off of my desk.

"Exactly what I said. He was watching your ass the whole time we walked down the hallway."

A flash of heat scored me, but I ignored it.

"Um, I think you're crazy. No way was Jesse Franklin checking out my ass."

"Way," Rachel countered with a grin. "He totally was."

"So what? He's my patient and the last thing I have time

for is anything related to romance."

Rachel rolled her eyes. "You know Dr. Johnson met his wife here in the clinic, right? We're almost in the middle of nowhere, and the only thing you've treated Jesse for is a dislocated shoulder. Get over it."

I reached her side, curling my hand around the doorknob. "I have a niece and a mother to take care of and that's my whole life."

Opening the door, I brushed past her. She called out after me. "Yeah, well maybe it would be good to expand your horizons."

I didn't reply because I couldn't. I didn't want to be rude, but I needed to go, or the tears pressing hot at the backs of my eyes and the emotion tightening my throat would let loose. Hurrying down the hallway, I mentally ran through what I needed to pick up at the grocery store before racing home as fast as possible.

Jesse Franklin, whether or not he had been staring at my ass, wasn't a man I could consider. I barely had time for fantasies. Not to mention, if he knew anything about my crazy life, he'd run far and fast in the opposite direction. Any sane man would.

Coming soon!
Sweet Fire

If you love steamy, small town romance, take a visit to Diamond Creek, Alaska in my Last Frontier Lodge Series. A sexy, alpha SEAL meets his match with a brainy heroine in Take Me Home. Don't miss Gage & Marley's story!

Go here to sign up for information on new releases: http://jhcroixauthor.com/subscribe/

Into The Fire Series

Burn For Me
Slow Burn
Burn So Bad
Hot Mess
Burn So Good
Sweet Fire
Play With Fire
Melt With You
Burn For You
Crash & Burn
Swoon Series
This Crazy Love
Wait For Me
Break My Fall
Brit Boys Sports Romance
The Play
Big Win
Out Of Bounds
Play Me
Naughty Wish
Diamond Creek Alaska Novels
When Love Comes
Follow Love
Love Unbroken
Love Untamed
Tumble Into Love
Christmas Nights
Last Frontier Lodge Novels
Take Me Home
Love at Last
Just This Once
Falling Fast
Stay With Me
When We Fall
Hold Me Close
Crazy For You

Catamount Lion Shifters

Protected Mate

Chosen Mate

Fated Mate

Destined Mate

A Catamount Christmas

Ghost Cat Shifters

The Lion Within

Lion Lost & Found

ACKNOWLEDGMENTS

To my readers—every single one of you. It's a honor to have you read my books. Your notes make my day. Thank you, thank you for making it possible for me to keep writing stories!

My proofreader angels swoop in to make sure I don't miss anything - Janine, Beth P., Terri D., Terri E., Heather H., & Carolyne B. - hugs! Yoly Cortez continues to create absolutely stunning covers for this series.

My husband cheers me on, makes me laugh, and keeps me grounded in this crazy journey of life.

xoxo

J.H. Croix